35995

P7

In the Morning

D1434314

Other novels by Michael Cronin

Against the Day
Through the Night

In the Morning

Michael Cronin

OXFORD
UNIVERSITY PRESS

For my mum

OXFORD
UNIVERSITY PRESS

Great Clarendon Street, Oxford OX2 6DP

Oxford University Press is a department of the University of Oxford.
It furthers the University's objective of excellence in research, scholarship,
and education by publishing worldwide in

Oxford New York

Auckland Cape Town Dar es Salaam Hong Kong Karachi
Kuala Lumpur Madrid Melbourne Mexico City Nairobi
New Delhi Shanghai Taipei Toronto

With offices in

Argentina Austria Brazil Chile Czech Republic France Greece
Guatemala Hungary Italy Japan Poland Portugal Singapore
South Korea Switzerland Thailand Turkey Ukraine Vietnam

Oxford is a registered trade mark of Oxford University Press
in the UK and in certain other countries

© Michael Cronin 2005

The moral rights of the author have been asserted

Database right Oxford University Press (maker)

First published 2005

All rights reserved. No part of this publication may be reproduced,
stored in a retrieval system, or transmitted, in any form or by any means,
without the prior permission in writing of Oxford University Press,
or as expressly permitted by law, or under terms agreed with the appropriate
reprographics rights organization. Enquiries concerning reproduction
outside the scope of the above should be sent to the Rights Department,
Oxford University Press, at the address above

You must not circulate this book in any other binding or cover
and you must impose this same condition on any acquirer

British Library Cataloguing in Publication Data

Data available

ISBN-10: 0-19-275447-5
ISBN-13: 978-0-19-275447-9

3 5 7 9 10 8 6 4 2

Typeset in Plantin by Palimpsest Book Production Ltd, Polmont, Stirlingshire

Printed in Great Britain by Cox & Wyman Ltd, Reading, Berkshire

Wiltshire, February 1945

The dawn came slowly that morning. But by eight o'clock it was light enough to put away the oil-lamps.

The man in the signal box yawned and stretched himself wearily. There was one more transport to see through the section and then he could go home to bed. He reached for his thermos flask and poured the last of the tea into his cup. It was grey and cold—like the morning itself.

The sky above the Downs was the colour of ash, and a thick mist filled the meadows on either side of the steep embankment which carried the line out of the cutting and east along the valley.

The bell on the wall above sounded insistently. The signalman put down his cup and stepped forward to his levers. It was then that he noticed the figure at the end of the cutting. He frowned. That wasn't Ted Chilcott: Ted Chilcott was supposed to be relieving him but that wasn't Ted. He secured the setting-lever and hauled number three and number five into place. Then he glanced down the line again to confirm that the signal had lifted to green. And was surprised to see that the stranger had gone.

Oh, he'd gone, right enough. He'd gone most of the way up the telegraph-pole. And when he reached the top he took out what looked like a pair of pliers and began to cut through the wires.

'Hold on! Just you hold on a minute!'

The signalman grabbed his hat and started for the stairs. But as he did so the door of the signal box opened. His visitor was a young man in a faded RAF greatcoat; his head and most of his face were covered by a woollen

1

balaclava. He placed a hand on the signalman's chest. In his other hand he held a large revolver.

'Nothing to get excited about, old boy,' he said. 'I'd stay put if I were you.'

The signalman stepped back against the wall.

'That's the ticket. Matter of fact, it'd be quite helpful if you stood a little closer to the window. Don't want the Jerries to get suspicious, do we?'

The rising scream of the whistle came first; then the roar, as train, steam, and smoke burst from the tunnel's mouth. The signal box shook beneath them as the powerful locomotive thundered by. In its wake came five military transporters. On each of them, draped in camouflage netting, was a Panzer IV: the Wehrmacht's deadly Tiger tank.

'Always on time,' said the man in the balaclava. He gestured towards the door: 'I think you and I had better be making a move.'

'But once they've gone through I'm supposed to write it in the book,' said the signalman.

'Not much point, old boy. I'm going to have to blow this place up. After you.'

The signalman grabbed his flask and made his way hurriedly down the wooden stairs.

His visitor followed. 'And now,' he said, when they reached the bottom, 'my advice to you would be to make yourself scarce.'

'Oh, right . . .' stammered the signalman, 'right you are.'

The masked man took a hand grenade from his pocket. He removed the pin and lobbed the grenade through the open door of the signal box.

The signalman heard the explosion but didn't look back. And he had almost reached the top of the cutting when he heard the second one. He turned and stood open-mouthed: as the train rounded the curve of the embankment, he saw it lift from the rails and launch itself into the mist below. Dark figures came swarming up on either side of the track and the silence of the morning was shattered by the staccato chatter of automatic fire. The soldiers in the guard-truck at the rear of the train were struggling to bring their machine-gun to bear; but before they could do so, truck, gun, and soldiers were dragged down the embankment with the rest of the speeding wreck.

'Well, I'll be—!'

The signalman turned and found Ted Chilcott standing by the gate above. 'Did you see that, Ted?' he said.

'I did,' came the reply. 'And blessed if I've ever seen the like.'

'Nor me neither.'

'Still, that's a few more won't be going home to help Hitler and his pals. You all right, Reg?'

The signalman shook his head. 'I dunno. It was . . . it was just like a dream and that's a fact.'

'How d'you mean?'

'They come out of nowhere. Ah, and that's where they've gone back to.'

The two men stood looking east along the empty track. The train and its attackers had sunk without trace beneath the sea of white mist.

'Like a lot of ghosts.'

'Thee go on, Reg Simmons! They en't no ghosts—they're men. Brave men and all. Come on, we better get off out of it.'

'Wait!'

'What?'

'Look!' The signalman pointed. 'There—on the slope!'

'Well I'm jiggered!'

The rising sun had cleared the crest, and its rays, slanting down through a gap in the hurrying clouds, were travelling across the other side of the valley. Four years earlier, in the weeks prior to the Invasion, the ancient landmark carved into the chalk there had been covered to prevent it giving help to enemy aircraft. Now, there it was, restored, a pale outline on the winter grass: an enormous prancing horse with its head thrown back and its forelegs raised, ready, it seemed, at any moment to gallop out of the earth.

3

Chapter 1

The vicious crack of the pistol-shot seemed to fill the darkened room. At the foot of the stairs, the young man with the pencil-line moustache called out in pain and threw his hand to his heart. His other hand clutched frantically at the newel-post. Then, slowly, his fingers lost their grip and he slid to the floor.

His assassin, a portly man in a voluminous tweed overcoat and pork-pie hat, remained expressionless. He placed the pistol on the table and sat down in the armchair next to the hearth. Almost at once, the headlights of a car swept past the window and the vehicle could be heard skidding to a halt on the gravel outside. Urgent footsteps approached the door.

And the curtain began to fall.

It rose again quickly and the dozen or so spectators, scattered across the stalls, applauded politely as the actors lined up along the footlights. The curtain fell once more, and it was over. The house-lights came on and the audience began to shuffle out.

By that time the man in the pork-pie hat was already hurrying along the corridor which led to the stage door. Two stagehands who were manoeuvring a large sofa down some stairs stepped aside to let him pass; then stepped aside again as, wiping the moustache from his upper lip, the young man came hurrying after him.

'Selwyn? Selwyn?' the young man called.

'Must dash, dear boy,' replied the overcoated figure. And with a nod to the stage-door keeper he pushed through into the rainswept evening.

But his pursuer caught up with him on the steps outside. 'Selwyn,' he said breathlessly, 'Selwyn, listen to me—if you fire that damned gun any closer you're going to take my ear off.'

'Nonsense.'

'It isn't nonsense!'

The man in the hat sighed. 'It can't do you any harm, Connors, it's only a blank. Which, to be perfectly frank, chimes rather well with the rest of your performance this afternoon. Now, if you'll excuse me, I'm in quest of a pint.' And, turning up his collar, he splashed away in the direction of the street.

The young man swore softly, and was about to go back inside when a hand touched him on the sleeve. 'Mr Connors?'

It was a boy of about fifteen. And he was proffering an autograph book.

'It is you, isn't it, Mr Connors?' said the boy.

Douglas Connors smiled. 'Yes, as a matter of fact, it is. Were you in for the matinée?'

'Could you write: "To Herbert Sillitoe, who recalls your Troubled Dane with lasting pleasure"?'

The actor frowned. 'Could I write what?'

'It's for my uncle.'

'Your uncle?' Connors hesitated. 'Oh, your uncle! I see. Yes, of course. Just a moment.'

'Do you want to use my pencil?' said the boy. 'It's indelible.'

'Is it? Is it really? No,' said the actor quickly, coming down the steps, 'no, there'll be no need for that.' He fumbled inside his jacket. 'You see, I've a particularly reliable pen of my own. By the by, I hope your uncle has no objection to royal-blue ink?'

'Not that I know of,' said the boy.

'That's good.' The actor scrawled hastily across the open page. 'There. How's that?'

'Thanks.'

The boy stuffed the book back into his pocket and walked

5

away up the alley which led to the street. Connors watched him thoughtfully, and then pushed open the door and went inside.

In shop windows all along the High Street assistants were pulling down the blinds and preparing to close up for the day. The pavements were busy. The boy stood for a moment watching the weary faces hurrying past. Even the prospect of liberation didn't seem to cheer them up. After four long years of Occupation prospects were not enough. They would believe in Liberation on the day it came marching up the street behind a brass band and not a moment before.

But that day was coming. For instance, the enormous 'V' for Victory daubed on the wall outside the Regal Cinema had been there for weeks. Not so long ago the Nasties would have had that wiped away in a matter of hours. And they would have done much the same to the people who'd painted it there if they could have got their hands on them. And they usually could. But now, with the Americans sweeping through Northern France and the Russians advancing inexorably from the East, the German Forces of Occupation had more important things to think about. Things like saving their skins.

The rain began to ease and a watery moon appeared between the broken clouds. It was no more than ten minutes walk back to the house. But you never went straight back. That was one of the first lessons you learned. Those who didn't sometimes never got back at all.

When he pushed open the door 'Uncle' Herbert Sillitoe was standing by the stove warming a saucepan of milk. He was a tall, pre-occupied looking man, who, even indoors, wore an overcoat and scarf against the cold. It was said he'd been a professor at one of the famous universities. He was clever, there was no doubt about that. And he was the best organizer for miles around. He'd held the South Midlands together through some of the worst of times.

'Ah, there you are, Eric,' he said.

It still sounded odd when he heard himself called that. But that was the name on his identity-card: Eric, Eric

Sampson. And on his ration-card, which was another skilful forgery. It seemed ages since anyone had called him by his real name. If it was his real name any more.

'Success?'

'I'm not sure.' He pulled the autograph book from his pocket.

'Uncle' Herbert took the book and walked over to the table. He flicked through the pages and slipped a narrow strip of paper from between them.

''Struth!' said the boy. 'I didn't see him put that there.'

'Connors knows his business. He's one of my most reliable couriers.' 'Uncle' Herbert took a magnifying-glass from his pocket and ran it along the paper strip. He nodded to himself then screwed the paper up and tossed it into the makeshift fire flickering in the grate. 'Listen, Eric,' he said, 'I had a visitor this afternoon. I've news for you.'

'For me?'

'You're needed elsewhere. To help with a printing-press. It's not far from Swindon.'

'I had an auntie lived in Swindon. And two cousins.'

'Uncle' Herbert frowned. 'Is there any likelihood you'd be recognized?'

'No. They moved to Sussex. To the village where I used to live. To Shevington. The last time I saw them—'

'Hell's bells!' 'Uncle' Herbert jumped up from the table and ran to the stove where the milk was boiling over furiously. 'Oh, well,' he said, holding the dripping saucepan aloft, 'I suppose it disguises the taste of the wretched stuff. I'm quite sure it's never seen the inside of a cow. Now listen, you're to go to Gifford's Mill. They'll be expecting you.'

'Gifford's Mill?'

'It's a flour mill. It's in a town called Charborough. You'll have to leave first thing in the morning.'

His bag was packed and ready. It always was. A small haversack containing a few items of clothing. But nothing that could give him away. Nothing personal. Like his name, he'd long ago lost the few personal things he'd once possessed.

7

He stretched out on the sofa and lay looking up at the ceiling with its familiar network of cracks and peeling distemper. He had worked for 'Uncle' Herbert Sillitoe for almost three months. 'Uncle' Herbert's was the most recent in a long line of Resistance cells to which he had been attached. The casualty rate in some groups, especially in the cities, had been remorseless.

He had worked for the Resistance for two years. Two life and death years of deceit and constant danger. But he had survived.

'And do'st tha know why?'

Who was it had asked him that? Wasn't it that miner—the one who'd been leader of the group near Leeds?

'Because th'ast an honest face. Not like this rogue.' And he'd laughed and pointed at Les.

And Les had laughed.

The two boys had been kept together in those early days. Him and Les Gill. He'd been glad of that. And he knew Les had too. After all, their friendship was a close one. And you didn't make many friends. Not in times like these. It wasn't wise. Friends could walk out of the door and never be seen again. And, of course, even friends could betray you. The Gestapo knew how to make people talk.

Where was Les now? And what was it they'd changed his name to? Tulliver . . . Ray Tulliver, that was it! And what about Mr Thrale? What was his . . . ? No, it was no good, he couldn't remember the new name Alec Thrale had been issued with. Besides, how many other names would he have been given since? Where were Les Gill and Alec Thrale now? he wondered. And what about everyone in Shevington? What had happened to them?

He closed his eyes. And where was his dad? It seemed a lifetime since the night in September 1940 when they had waved goodbye: the night the Germans landed. He wondered if . . .

But what was the point of wondering? Wondering didn't get you anywhere. The war had changed everything. The coming of the Nasties had ransacked everyone's life and nothing was the same any more.

'Eric!'

He heard a chair scrape and opened his eyes to see 'Uncle' Herbert getting up from the table.

'What?'

'Uncle' Herbert put his finger to his lips. He went over to the window and drew back the edge of the curtain. 'Oh, dear!' he said quietly. 'Get up, Eric!'

'What?'

'We've got visitors. Out with you! Now! And take care. They'll be watching the street. Quickly!'

Eric scrambled to his feet and grabbed his haversack. When he reached the door he looked back. 'Uncle' Herbert had taken a pistol from the drawer and was ramming an ammunition-clip into place.

'Don't wait for me, boy,' he said. 'Go on!'

'But . . .'

'Close the door and get out!'

He clambered up onto the banister, lifted the attic hatch, and hauled himself inside. Almost at once he heard running footsteps in the stairwell below. Crouched above them, scarcely daring to breathe, he heard their shouts, and then the sound of the door being broken down. And then the shooting began.

It didn't last long.

How long he wasn't sure. The shooting was followed by the sound of breaking crockery and muffled conversation. Then, suddenly, there were footsteps on the stairs, shouts from the street and car doors slamming. They hadn't bothered with anyone else in the building. They had known exactly which room to go to.

He lifted the edge of the hatch an inch or two. 'Uncle' Herbert's door was hanging from its hinges. The saucepan and its contents lay in a grey puddle on the linoleum. The table and chairs had been overturned and the cupboards thrown open. The Gestapo had been looking for something. But 'Uncle' Herbert was a careful man. They probably hadn't found it. But they had found him. There was blood on the threadbare carpet at the top of the stairs.

He heard a door opening on the floor below and a voice called tentatively: 'Is there anything wrong?' The neighbours were stirring.

His route was the one 'Uncle' Herbert had insisted he rehearse time and time again: across the attic, through the hole in the party-wall, and down into the flats next door. Then down the stairs, out of the back door, and up the alley. At the end of the alley he stopped and carefully checked the street beyond. It was empty apart from two men coming out of a nearby pub and another man waiting at the bus stop. He shouldered his haversack and walked away.

Should he head for the outskirts and try and pick up a lift? Or make for the railway station? Most of the trains had been commandeered to carry the remaining divisions of the Wehrmacht to the coast. Berlin was calling its legions home. And besides, railway stations were a magnet for Gestapo agents. No—the other side of the city was his best option.

He walked quickly but not too quickly. Not quickly enough to draw attention to himself. After a while he even found time to stop and look in a shop window. It was a sweet shop. Or, at least, it had been. A melancholy jar of liquorice-sticks was all that remained, high on one dusty shelf. The glance he gave it was brief, but long enough to be certain. Yes—he was still there. Reflected in the glass. There on the other side of the street. The same one who'd been there last time he'd looked. The one in the trench coat and workman's cap. It was the man who'd been standing at the bus stop near 'Uncle' Herbert's.

He fought the instinct to run. You always wanted to run. But that could be fatal. When you were being followed you never let on you knew you were. Find crowds quickly and lose yourself! That's what everyone said. The market square was his only hope.

These last weeks, as the chaos of the German withdrawal

had become more and more apparent, the town centre was even busier after dark than it was during the day. As night fell, the high street and the square became a nightmare image of what they were during daylight hours. The patient queues that filled the pavements from morning to dusk were replaced by milling, desperate crowds, by arguments and whispers, by the buying and selling of anything and everything that could be bought and sold.

'Need some insurance?' said a man in a long overcoat. A strange banknote appeared between his fingers. 'Yankee dollar?' he said, flourishing it like a magician. 'Be prepared, eh, son? Like the Boy Scouts.'

Elsewhere, from suitcases which snapped open and closed like hungry teeth, butter and sugar and tea could be obtained by anyone with something to offer other than the worthless official banknotes with their celebration of Hitler's victories—Warsaw, Amsterdam, Paris, London— on one side, and the glowering portrait of the Führer himself, the Great Leader, on the other.

When he reached the far corner of the square he risked one quick look back. And breathed a long sigh of relief. It had worked. There was no sign of his pursuer. Now all he had to do was slip away down one of the side streets. He waited on the pavement as some buskers shuffled past. The one with the harmonica held out a cap containing a few copper coins. The one in front, the one with the trumpet, had a piece of cardboard hanging round his neck. Pencilled on it was the word: EX-SERVICEMEN. The buskers moved on and he was about to step from the kerb when a voice said:

'You reckoned you'd shook me off, didn't you?'

He felt his shoulders stiffen. The speaker was only a few feet away. There was no point trying to run. Not unless he was looking for a bullet in the back. He turned slowly.

His pursuer stepped from a nearby doorway. 'Led me a proper dance, you have,' he said.

'Me? What're you talking about?'

'You're good, I'll say that,' said the stranger, pushing

back his cap and coming forward into the light. 'But not that good.'

'I don't know what . . . Who . . . ?' The face beneath the cap was suddenly familiar. So familiar! But it couldn't be. No! He shook his head in disbelief. 'Les? Les Gill? It's not, is it?'

'Well, it was last time I looked. How're you doing, Frank Tate?'

Chapter 2

'Les!'

'I'd have known that trilby hat of yours anywhere.'

'Les, I thought . . . I thought you were a Gestapo nark, coming after me like that!'

'Just keeping an eye on you. Making sure you wasn't being followed.'

'Les Gill!' The boys shook hands enthusiastically. 'Les Gill, am I glad to see you!'

'Likewise. Fancy a cup of something? I've been travellin' all day.'

They found a dingy, steam-filled café in a side street and took their cups to an empty table near the door.

'I was on my way to "Uncle" Herbert,' said Les.

'Les, "Uncle" Herbert's . . .'

'I know. I saw them drive away.'

'He was always so careful,' said Frank.

'They're going for anyone they can lay their hands on,' said Les. 'Like mad dogs.'

Frank shook his head. He still wasn't sure he could believe his eyes. 'Les Gill,' he said. 'Where have you been? What have you been doing?'

'This and that. Plenty of that!' Les drew his finger across his throat dramatically. 'What about you?'

'Oh, you know, here and there.'

'Whatever we've been doing, it looks like it's made men of us, ain't it? Ain't that what they say?'

'We're still here, Les. Wait—wasn't it Ray! Wasn't that what they changed you to?'

'And I've had plenty of other names since. Ain't we all?

Nah—it wouldn't feel right you calling me anything but Les.'

'Me neither!' said Frank. 'Me being Frank, I mean.'

And they both laughed.

'Listen, any news of your dad?' said Les.

'Dad? No,' said Frank, 'nothing.'

'You've still got no idea where he is?'

Frank shook his head. 'I don't think about it any more. Well, not much. What about you? Heard anything from Shevington? Anything from Mill and—'

But Les interrupted him. 'Keep your voice down,' he said. And glanced quickly round the tables. 'They've got people everywhere, know what I mean? Listen, we've got to work out what to do.'

'I've got to go south,' said Frank. 'But what're you going to do?'

'I'm coming with you.'

'Straight up?'

'There's nothing for me here. Not now "Uncle" Herbert's been took.'

'You and me, Les! It'll be like the old days! Remember?'

Les shrugged and blew on his tea.

That wary look, which had been Les Gill's reaction to most things when Frank had first known him back in Shevington, seemed to have settled on him permanently. Les obviously wasn't in the mood to do much remembering, but their meeting had brought the memories crowding back for Frank. Shevington held so many memories. Shevington was where he had gone after his father disappeared at the beginning of the war. He had lived in the small Sussex village with his grandmother, Nan Tate, and his aunt Edith and his cousins, Colin and Rose, in Nan's crowded cottage. Les Gill and his sister, Mill, the two Cockney evacuees, had been his only friends. Frank Tate and Les Gill had been inseparable from the day they'd met. And had remained so until the spring of '43. That was the year resistance to the invaders had really begun. That was the year they had been forced to leave Shevington far behind.

'Remember, Les? Remember how we always wanted to get back at the Nasties? To have a go at them? Well, we have. They're beaten, Les.'

'They ain't beat yet, Frank.'

'They will be. We've just got to keep going.'

'"Consider Garibaldi", eh?'

'Les, fancy you rememberin' that! Yes, "Consider Garibaldi!"'

'That's what your gran used to say.'

'That's what Nan Tate always used to say. Cos Garibaldi never gave up. Remember when . . . '

'Forget it, Frank.' Les picked up his bag and started for the door. 'We ain't got time.'

Frank took a last, hurried mouthful of tea and followed him out.

What worthless and disordered lives these people led!

Reinhardt Schilte wrinkled his nose in disgust as he surveyed the shabby room. He missed nothing: the hint of drains coming from the sink, the bottle of black-market whisky on the shelf, the faded silk dressing-gown on the back of the door, and the worn sticks of greasepaint on the towel in front of the peeling mirror. He took special note of the greasepaint. He had already taken note of the actor's jacket which was thrown across the back of the chair—and had searched its pockets.

There was the sound of applause from somewhere outside and Schilte looked at his watch. Time was getting on. He had other arrests to make that evening.

Douglas Connors opened the door, threw down his hat, and was reaching for the whisky bottle when he glanced in the mirror and caught sight of the figure in the broken armchair beside the sink.

'Who the—?'

'Good evening, Mr Connors,' said his visitor. 'Schilte, Reinhardt Schilte. Gestapo.'

'May I ask what you're doing here?'

'You must excuse me. But as I was in the vicinity . . . well, you knew that, of course.'

'What do you mean?' said the actor.

Schilte smiled. 'We have waited a long time to dispose of Mr Sillitoe. However, it is better late then never! That is an English expression, I think?'

'*Than* never. Yes, it is.'

'*Than* never. Thank you, Mr Connors. Sillitoe will not be bothering us again.'

'And the boy?'

'The boy?' Schilte frowned. 'What boy?'

'It was a boy who came to pick up the information this evening. He came to the stage door. But look here,' said the actor, sitting down suddenly, 'there's something I need to discuss with you rather urgently.'

'You will, of course, receive your usual payment.'

'It's not that. What I want to ask you about is . . . well, the arrangements.'

'Arrangements?'

'It's perfectly clear what's happening. Your lot are clearing out and doing so pretty damned fast.'

'The armies of the Reich are regrouping, Mr Connors. In order to deal more effectively with the Americans and their Bolshevik allies.'

'Quite. And meanwhile . . . '

'We won't forget our friends.'

'Ah! That's just it, you see. I won't be very popular when the people here—Sillitoe's people—find out what I've been up to. And they will find out. One shouldn't underestimate them.'

'Loyal servants of the Reich will not be forgotten.'

'There'll be a seat, then?'`

'A seat?'

'On the last plane out?'

Schilte smiled. 'That is a rather dramatic way of putting it. But rest assured everything and everyone will be taken care of.'

'I'm relieved to hear it. Very relieved. Can I offer you a drink?'

'Thank you, no.' Schilte watched the actor pour the whisky into the glass. Then, 'Tell me, Mr Connors,' he said, indicating the stubs of make-up; 'these cosmetics . . . '

'The greasepaints? Tools of the trade. What about them?'

'I was wondering, if it were necessary, could you paint a face other than your own?'

'How do you mean?'

'Could you make-up a face that was not your own?'

'Yes, of course. Why do you ask?'

'Gauleiter Müller, Mr Connors . . . '

Connors stared at him. 'Gauleiter Müller?'

'You know the name, of course.'

'Of course. Doesn't everyone? He's been running most of the country for the last four years.'

'The Gauleiter is being recalled to Berlin. For consultations. I must deliver him to a discreet airstrip. And, naturally, I wish to do so unobserved. I don't need to tell you what encouragement it would give our enemies to learn that the Gauleiter was leaving Britain—even temporarily. I'd prefer there to be no possibility, none whatsoever, of his being recognized. By anyone. Even accidentally. Do you follow me?'

'D'you mean . . . Do you mean make him up? Disguise him?'

'That is precisely what I mean. It would put your skills to worthwhile use, don't you think?'

'The full fig? Wig, moustache—that sort of thing?'

'That would be for you to decide. Rest assured we would not be ungrateful.'

'Of course not. I mean, I'm more than happy to oblige, Herr Schilte. Gauleiter Müller! It would be a privilege. But when? We're moving theatres at the end of the week, you see. Off to our next venue.'

Schilte smiled. 'Have no fear, Mr Connors; when I need you I will find you.' The Gestapo commander stood up. 'No, don't disturb yourself; I can see myself out.' He placed a wedge of banknotes beside Connors's glass and walked to the door. 'By the way,' he said, 'what did he look like— this boy who came to see you this evening?'

'The boy?' Connors was eyeing the banknotes: they were American dollars, counterfeit probably. 'He was just a boy,' he said, 'I can't say I actually took much notice.'

'What a pity. Well, no matter.'

The Gestapo agent closed the door and Douglas Connors reached for the bottle and poured himself another drink.

He had hardly done so when the door opened again and a smiling face appeared under a pork-pie hat.

'Close enough for you, Connors?'

Connors hastily covered the banknotes with his towel. 'Oh, it's you, Selwyn. Sorry?' he said. 'What do you mean "close enough"?'

'The pistol shot?'

'Oh, that. No problem at all.'

'Good. I must say I thought Act Three went rather well tonight, didn't you? Coming for a pint?'

'Thanks all the same. I'm feeling rather tired.'

'So I see. I've never been one for drinking alone, myself. Goodnight.'

'Close enough? Far too close!' said Connors softly as the door closed. How long had Selwyn been outside? Now it would be all over the theatre that the German had been in his room. He stuffed the dollar bills into his pocket. Still, this Müller business could be the answer to everything. Yes, indeed! Rather a good mast to which to pin your colours, Douglas! Especially in times like these. Connors lifted his glass to the face in the mirror.

'Your health, dear boy!'

Frank and Les had been walking most of the night when they came across the van. It had skidded off the road. The driver offered them a lift if they'd help him push it out of the ditch. It was urgent, he told them. Very urgent. They decided it might be wise not to enquire what was in the back of the van. And they were soon sitting beside him and heading south. Les immediately fell asleep, and Frank, after a few desultory attempts at conversation, found to his relief that the driver was too busy negotiating the dark road to talk much.

Night-time was the time for journeys. The burnt-out troop-carriers and the wrecked and abandoned weaponry beside the road were evidence of the dangers of travelling by day. American fighter planes were strafing anything that moved, even this distance from the coast.

As they drove along, the hooded headlights would occasionally pick out a solitary walker, suitcase in hand; or sometimes a group of women and children pushing prams piled with luggage: pale figures emerging like spectres from the gloom. Spectres that seldom acknowledged the vehicle creeping by but pressed on determinedly, saving all their energy for the miles ahead of them.

The van made good progress and they had been travelling steadily for almost half an hour when, without any warning, the driver stamped on the brake and threw both boys forward against the dashboard.

'What was that for?' said Les angrily, blinking himself awake and rubbing his forehead.

The driver did not reply. They followed his anxious gaze to the group of men standing by the trees where the road swung away to the right. There were half a dozen of them. Wehrmacht stragglers. Dishevelled and tired looking. When they saw the stationary van two of the soldiers immediately ran towards it.

'*Halt!*' they called. 'You! Get out! Get out, all of you!'

The driver was trembling as he opened his door. Frank and Les got out slowly on the other side. Several of the soldiers had meanwhile gone round to the back of the van and were prising open the doors.

'*Schaut mal,*' one of them called. '*Zigaretten!*'

'*Macht Platz!*' replied the sergeant who was with them. And they began to pull the boxes out onto the road. The sergeant turned to the driver. 'Over there,' he said. 'Stand by the ditch.' He motioned to Frank and Les. 'And you two stand beside him.'

19

With his hands in the air the driver began to plead with the soldier. 'Take the fags,' he begged him. 'And the van. Take them. I don't care. Take the lot.'

'I will do so.'

'All right, all right. But just leave me alone, eh? Just let me go? I mean, what's the point?'

But the sergeant was already drawing a pistol from inside his tunic.

When he saw this the driver gave a low moan, dropped to his knees and began to shuffle forwards. It was a chance—and Les took it. He kicked at the kneeling man with all his might and sent him crashing against the soldier. The pistol went off and the two men fell in a heap. Frank and Les scrambled desperately up the bank and through the hedge into the darkness beyond. As they stumbled across the field on the other side there were shouts and a second shot. But it seemed that the soldiers were more interested in the van than the escapers. And not long after, the engine coughed to life and they heard it drive away.

'Les,' said Frank breathlessly, 'that was close!'

Les grinned and sat down. 'Like old times, eh?'

And Frank laughed and collapsed on the ground beside him.

They were silent for a moment or two getting their breath back. Then:

'Listen, Frank,' said Les, '. . . before . . . you know, when we were in the caff . . . I didn't mean to be so short with you . . . Fact is, I don't like rememberin', see? Not about Shevington.'

'You remembered "Consider Garibaldi!"'

'I know. But what I'm saying is there wasn't no need for me to be so short with you.'

'Forget it.'

'No. I owe you. You saved my life, Frank—the day we attacked the convoy, remember?'

'You don't owe me, Les. And what about Mr Thrale? And poor old Sims?'

'No, you was the one, Frank. They helped but you was

the one. You've always been my best pal. You and Mill was my best pals. I can't afford to lose you and all.'

'Les, it's me and you again. That's all that matters. Like the old days, eh?'

'We was kids then, Frank. It's different when you're a kid. When you're a kid you don't understand what's really happening, do you? Or what could happen. Everything just sort of . . . just sort of happens to you.'

'I s'pose.'

'Me and Mill was kids together . . . ' Les stopped. Why? Why did all roads lead back to Mill?

'What is it?' said Frank.

'Frank, I en't never forgive myself. That . . . that thing I done to Mill . . . when I left Shevington . . . that's the worst thing I've ever done.'

'Les, she knew you didn't mean it; she knew that.'

'But I did, Frank, I did mean it. That's the trouble.'

'It was the way it looked, Les. You can't blame yourself.'

'I can. And so does she. I know she does.'

Les turned his face away. He'd said enough. He hadn't planned to come out with that stuff about his sister, Mill. But it had been easy to talk in the darkness. Easier to say things. Hard things. And, of course, it was easier because it was Frank he was saying it to. Frank knew all about what had happened with Mill. About the young Jerry. And the hidden radio. All of it. Frank was his mate. He still was. Les hadn't thought that would matter—so many things didn't matter any more—but that did.

'I'm really pleased to see you again, Frank.'

'Likewise, Les. And we're going to see the Nasties beaten—me and you. Consider Garibaldi!'

'Consider Garibaldi!'

To risk themselves to the dark fields would have meant getting lost good and proper. So they walked on following the road for a mile or two. But then a glow in the sky to the east made them stop.

'Bit early for morning,' said Les.

'That ain't morning,' said Frank. 'Look.'

21

As they drew closer to the top of the hill the glow became more intense, silhouetting the bare treetops in its glare.

When they reached the crest they found that a Wehrmacht fuel-tender had slewed sideways and was jammed across the road following a collision with a civilian car. The car was on fire. The driver of the fuel-tender was struggling frantically to reverse it away; and a soldier in a forage cap was trying to restore order among a group of travellers who had stopped beside the blaze unable to proceed up or down the hill.

''Struth,' said Les. 'If that lot goes up . . . '

'Stay here,' said Frank. 'I'll find out if there's a way round it.'

The car was blazing steadily but no one seemed to know what to do about it. People were standing about, watching the flames. Some had put down their cases and others were sitting wearily by the roadside as though they had reached journey's end. The driver of the fuel-tender continued his efforts to reverse his vehicle but the engine seemed to have seized up. Despite desperate encouragement from the soldier in the forage cap the driver couldn't move it and the tender remained exactly where it was, side-on across the road and only yards from the burning car.

Frank went up to a woman with a perambulator who was standing beside the hedge. The pram was piled so high with suitcases and boxes that it was impossible to tell whether there was a child inside.

'You ought to move away, you know,' he said.

'What?' she said. Her face was pale and her eyes ringed with dark shadows of fatigue.

'Everyone ought to get out of the way. And quickly.'

'I think that's what that German's trying to say,' she replied.

'Well, he's right. Is there a way through these hedges? Into the fields?'

'I don't know.'

Frank looked back up the hill towards Les and waved. Les returned the wave and started down towards him.

22

He saw the woman with the pram nodding at Frank. He saw her reach for the handle of the pram. And then he saw them look up. And Les looked up too. It came from the hills to the west, very low and very fast: a fighter-bomber. He could see the pale American star and roundel on its underwings caught in the glare of the burning car. And everyone began to run.

'Frank!' he yelled. And threw himself to the ground.

The fireball lit up the hillside and a muffled roar shook the earth as the aircraft roared overhead and bored its way into the darkness beyond.

When Les looked again the fuel-tender was blazing furiously. There were bodies strewn in the road all around it like dark bundles of rag. He picked himself up and stumbled on down the hill. The heat was overwhelming. He peered desperately into the flames unwilling and unable to believe his eyes. He felt someone grab his arm and try to drag him away. But he resisted, shaking his head, reaching forward and calling. 'Frank?' he called. 'Frank?'

'Don't be a fool,' said a voice. 'Come on! They'll be back to finish the job.'

'I can't,' he insisted, 'I can't just leave him.'

But a second hand gripped him by the other arm. 'There's nothing you can do. There's nobody going to come out of that. Run!'

Chapter 3

He had run. Like the rest of them. Away from the flames and into the safety of the dark fields.

It made no difference to him that what they'd said had been true. That the American plane had returned minutes later and machine-gunned what remained of the Wehrmacht fuel-truck; and that those bullets, raking the road and hedges, would certainly have killed him and anyone else still standing there. He had run. And left his friend on the hillside.

The two men who had dragged him clear, and three or four other travellers who had survived the attack, stayed together, walking south across country and eventually back to the main road. Les followed them, listening to their noisy and excited recollections of those awful moments of fire and death. But he said nothing. He had nothing to say. Remembering never helped anything. Not to Les's mind it didn't. That's how things were in wartime, wasn't it? Things happened. One minute you were there and the next . . . There was no point remembering. The thing to do was to keep moving. That was the trick.

It was beginning to get light when one of the two men dropped back and fell into step beside him.

'How you doing, friend?' he said. 'How's that hand?'

'What?'

'Your hand. You burnt yourself.'

Les looked down. There were two large blisters on the palm of his right hand. 'Yes,' he said.

'Where are you heading for?' the man asked. 'Only I'm cutting off at the next crossroads.'

24

'Charborough.'

'Charborough? You've got plenty of walking yet. Just keep going due south.'

'Thanks.'

Les watched him hurry away down the road. The others were moving off too. No one looked back.

As the first, metallic streaks of light appeared in the eastern sky he shouldered his bag and started south.

There were birds singing. And he could feel rain on his face.

He opened his eyes. He was sitting with his back against the trunk of a tree. It felt like morning; it felt as if he had been asleep.

'Oh, good,' said a voice, 'you're awake.'

He looked up blearily. It was a girl. She was what . . . eight? Nine years old? She wore a yellow beret and a tightly belted raincoat.

'What happened?' he asked.

'You were making little noises,' she said; 'so I dragged you over here. I think you must have been blown through the hedge.'

He seemed to have trouble hearing. And when he moved, the pain in his neck stabbed up into the back of his head.

'What's . . . what's that smell?'

'Petrol. I'm afraid your coat is torn and so is your shirt. But your hat stayed on. Isn't that odd?'

He touched the battered trilby. Yes—it was still there. 'It's my lucky hat,' he said. And tried to stand up, but his legs wouldn't support him.

'Hold on to me,' she said.

There was a big, black perambulator next to her. The paint along its side was blistered. For some reason he was sure he'd seen it somewhere before.

'Come on,' she said. 'Up you get!'

He tucked his knees underneath him, clinging to the trunk of the tree and dragging himself up until he was on his feet.

25

'Where's Les?' he asked. 'Where is he?' And then, suddenly, there was that pain in his head again and the earth rushed up to meet him.

Once or twice he seemed to surface from some deep, dark place, floating up through several levels of brightness until he reached daylight. And she was always there: a small, rather pointed face under the beret. She was pushing the pram and smiling down at him. Then, like ink in water, the darkness would come clouding up out of the depths and overwhelm him.

Until he opened his eyes and . . .

'You really were tired, weren't you,' she said.

'Where . . . where am I?'

'You're perfectly safe.' She plumped up the pillow behind his head. 'This used to be Nanny Gale's room. The facilities are through that door. And my room's through the other one.'

Dusty daylight filtered through the wooden shutters which had been secured across the window. It was a small room with bare walls, on which were outlined vacant spaces, ovals and rectangles, where paintings or photographs had once hung. He was lying on a narrow, iron-framed bed. Some blankets and a rug had been thrown over him. Beside the bed was a small table on which a bowl and pitcher of water had been placed; and on the other side stood the chair on which his rescuer was sitting.

'You walked up the stairs,' she said. 'I don't think your legs are hurt. It's probably just concussion.'

'I can't remember . . .'

'That's one of the symptoms.'

She was . . . ? Now he could see her more clearly perhaps she was a little older than he'd first thought. Ten years old? Under her yellow beret, her hair was straw-coloured and braided into a long plait which hung down over one shoulder. There was a book open in her lap.

'I've been keeping vigil,' she said. And got up. 'I expect you're hungry. Try not to move. And be as quiet as you can. I won't be long.'

He saw the door close behind her. And thought, but wasn't sure, that he heard a key turning.

She had left the book open face-down on the chair. He reached across and picked it up. It had a dark green cover with a raised design in gold depicting a group of knights in armour emerging from a wood. Its title read: *The Idylls of the King* by Alfred Tennyson. Inside the cover was a bookplate on which a careful hand had written:

Ex Libris
Hannah Gale

Simon Carey was in the gunroom when he heard the gong for lunch. He'd been counting the remaining shotgun cartridges. Ammunition was low but not disastrously so. He secured the drawer and hurried to the dining room. He always seemed to be hungry these days.

He sat down opposite his sister. And eyed her suspiciously.

Now why was she so prompt today? She was usually the last to arrive; and lately, more often than not, she didn't arrive at all. She did it to annoy, of course. It was yet another of her 'eccentricities'. Silly child. Father was far too busy to deal with her. And mother—he glanced along the table to where his mother sat with a book propped against the teapot, from which, from time to time, and without looking up, she filled her cup—lately, mother seemed to have washed her hands of her completely.

'Felicity!' he barked. His sister had carelessly tipped her plate sideways. Half her lunch had ended up on the carpet. 'You really are the end, Felicity!'

'There's no need to raise your voice,' she said. 'Your advantage of years gives you no right whatsoever to be unpleasant. Isn't that so, Daddy?'

'I daresay, darling,' her father replied abstractedly. 'But do take care. Waste not want not, you know.'

'See!' said Simon. And she made a face at him, which

he was far too adult to return. 'You were out early this morning,' he said.

'I might have been,' she replied. 'What of it?'

'You shouldn't leave the grounds, Felicity,' said her father. 'There are some very dangerous people on the loose, you know.'

'The sort that would kill you brutally,' said her brother. 'You do know that, don't you? They'd do it as soon as look at you.'

'I didn't see a soul,' she replied. 'Besides, I have more faith in human nature than you. You just take it for granted everyone's nasty.'

'One should never underestimate people's ability to hate, dear,' said her mother, without looking up from her book.

Mr Carey helped himself to more potatoes from the tureen. 'I thought I heard bombs again during the night,' he said.

'The Yanks are trying to block the roads,' Simon observed authoritatively; 'to keep troop movements to a minimum. They said so on the wireless.'

His father nodded. 'Now they've control of the airfields in Normandy they've certainly got the upper hand.'

'They sliced through France like a knife through butter.'

'But Germany will be a different matter, Simon, I don't think there's any question of that. By the way, anything to report from your rounds, old fellow?'

'Nothing of consequence, sir. There's some minor damage to the river copses, that's all. It looks as if the locals have been scavenging for kindling again.'

'But no sign of those types you saw in the lane the other afternoon?'

'None. The shotgun saw them off good and proper.'

'Good man. We must be especially careful. I know it's tiresome. But it won't be long now. Things are moving, and moving quite rapidly.'

The phone began to ring out in the hall and Mr Carey got up quickly. 'Leave it, Mrs Cato!' he called. 'I'll take it in the study.'

'Poor father,' said Simon. 'There's so much to organize. Felicity? Felicity, are you listening? You really are the limit. Everyone's jolly sick of the way you're carrying on, you know. If we don't pull together this family won't survive.'

'You're so predictable, Simon,' she replied.

'And you're so bally complacent!'

'Language.'

'Damn it all, Felicity! Have you any idea of what's happening to us? Have you any idea at all what's involved?'

'Why do you always try to sound so grown-up, Simon?' she said. 'You don't really expect anyone to take you seriously, do you? The sort of boy who spends his every waking hour looking for an old wishbone?'

'That wishbone is as much mine as it is yours!' he snapped. 'You know bally well it is . . .' And then he realized that he'd walked into her trap. 'Mother,' he exclaimed, 'mother, tell her!' But his mother didn't appear to have heard. 'I loathe you, Felicity Carey!' he hissed. 'But you'll see . . . you'll just bally well see!' And throwing down his napkin he stormed from the room.

The door slammed behind him. Felicity made sure that her mother was still engrossed in her book. Then she reached down and slipped the potatoes and fish into the pocket of her pinafore.

Les? What had happened to Les? He'd been far enough away from the fuel-tender to escape the explosion. Frank was sure that's what he remembered. There must be a good chance that he'd got away. Mustn't there? Afterwards . . .

It was no good. He couldn't remember. From the moment Frank had looked up and seen the plane . . . he'd even seen the pilot's face, he remembered that . . . everything was blank. He could remember nothing afterwards until he'd woken up next to the tree. With that girl.

She was sitting in the chair beside the bed. She hadn't noticed that he was awake. She was reading quietly to herself. It sounded like poetry.

'. . . and from them rose
A cry that shiver'd to the tingling stars,
And, as it were one voice, an agony
Of lamentation, like a wind that shrills
All night in a waste land, where no one comes,
Or hath come, since the making of the world.'

'Hannah?' he said. 'Hannah?'

She looked up. 'Oh, I'm sorry,' she said. 'I didn't realize you were awake.'

'It is Hannah, isn't it?'

'Hannah? No. Why do you say that? My name is Felicity. Felicity Winfred Carey. Look, I've brought you some lunch!' She took the potatoes and cold fish from her pinafore and placed them on the blanket. 'These will help you get your strength back.'

'Where are we?' he asked.

'Winscombe Court. Father bought it for my mother when they were married. He's rich, you see. And she's from very very ancient stock. You can tell by her strikingly blue eyes. I mean, lots of people have blue eyes but Mummy's are exceptional. When she was a girl people used to come from miles around just to look at her. Imagine!'

'And where is Winscombe Court?'

'It's in Wiltshire. We're not far from the Downs. You can actually see the famous White Horse from the roof. When you get better we can climb up to the leads and look at it together.' She hugged her book tightly to her. 'Oh, I'm so glad I found you!' she said. 'When I heard the bombs last night I hoped there might be survivors. And look what else I found!' She reached into the pocket of her pinafore and pulled out a Wehrmacht forage cap.

He watched as she slipped it on and arranged it at a jaunty angle. The cap was stained darkly all along one side. He frowned: there'd been a German soldier trying to direct the traffic on the hill, hadn't there?

'Where did you get that?' he said.

'Don't you like it?'

30

'It looks like . . . It doesn't matter. Listen,' he said, 'was I on my own? You know, when you found me?'

'Oh, yes. The others were all asleep.'

'You mean they were . . . ? Was there one about my age? A chap with . . . ?'

'You'll only tire yourself trying to remember things,' she said. 'You must save your strength, Eric.'

'How do you know my name?'

'From your identity-card.'

'Look . . .' Frank eased himself up on the pillow. And winced. His head hurt when he moved. 'I can't stay here,' he said.

'Of course, you can; I'm going to look after you.'

'Does anyone else know I'm here?'

'You needn't worry. I've no intention of telling my parents.'

'Why not?'

'I don't think they'd like you very much. You must get lots of sleep,' she said. And stood up suddenly. 'By the way, please don't try and open the shutters.'

She went out and Frank heard the key turning in the lock. 'Why are you locking the door?' he called.

'It's for your own good,' she replied. 'The house can be dangerous if you don't know your way around.'

It was late afternoon by the time Les reached the outskirts of the small market-town.

He stood looking up uncertainly at the derelict building with the faded lettering on its wall. He'd been expecting a windmill. It wasn't. Gifford's Mill was a tall, box-like structure with clapboard facing from which most of the paint had peeled. It seemed to be deserted; but as Les pushed open the gate a figure appeared in the doorway.

'Looking for someone?'

'Is this Gifford's?' called Les.

'It used to be,' the man replied, coming across the yard. 'But if it's flour you're looking for . . .'

31

'No, I ain't looking for flour.'

'No?'

'I've been sent.'

'Been "sent" have you?' said the man. And laughed. 'What—like in the Bible?'

'I've come to help.'

'We've got no vacancies, I'm afraid.'

'I'm Les Gill.'

'Is that a fact?'

'But that's not who you're expecting.'

'You've got the advantage of me. Who am I expecting?'

'Oh, for—' said Les angrily. 'His name's . . . his name's Eric, Eric Sampson.'

'No need to lose your rag. And where is he . . . this Eric Sampson?'

'He's dead!' Les heard himself shout. 'He's dead, all right? A Yank plane shot us up on the road and killed him. And his name wasn't Sampson, it was Frank, Frank Tate! He was my best mate. And . . . and . . .' His voice suddenly lost its anger. He felt dizzy; and he reached out to steady himself against the wall. 'He ain't here,' he said quietly, '. . . cos he's dead.'

The man took his arm. 'You'd better come inside,' he said.

Chapter 4

There had been a house on the hill at Winscombe for as long as records existed. And probably long before. It had been a Saxon hall, a Tudor grange, and an elegant Georgian country house. Then, finally, towards the end of the nineteenth century, it had been re-built as a sprawling, ivy-clad Victorian villa, with fine lawns and an imposing stand of elegaic elms. This was the house to which, in the spring of 1930, Hugh Carey had brought his bride, the former Rowena Filton-Bourne.

Hugh's family owned factories in the Midlands. They had done so for three generations. Rowena's fortunes sprang from more ancient stock. The roots of her family tree looked like one of those tangled thickets in which fairytale princesses are imprisoned and left to languish. Not that Rowena had ever languished. She was far too resourceful for that. After her father lost most of his money in the Wall Street Crash of 1929, Rowena Filton-Bourne had gone out into the world and looked for answers. And one of the answers she'd found had been Hugh Carey.

As soon as their engagement was announced, Rowena set about finding a suitable home for them. She had very decided opinions about what would be appropriate. But the afternoon she and her fiancé motored up the valley and saw Winscombe Court she knew at once that they need look no further. The purchase took only a matter of weeks, the house was quickly re-furnished, and the happy couple were able to take up residence not long after they returned, bronzed and enthusiastic, from their honeymoon in the Austrian Alps.

The years since had been among the most turbulent the Court had ever seen. Throughout the world there had been economic chaos as financial markets collapsed, industry plunged into what seemed terminal decline, and millions on millions of men and women were thrown into poverty and unemployment.

But life at Winscombe went on. There were the births of first a son and heir, Simon; and four years later, a daughter, Felicity Winfred. And whatever dark clouds might be gathering over Europe and however hard it was to ignore the sound of the approaching storm, Hugh and Rowena Carey's home began to acquire a reputation. There were, it was true, much grander houses elsewhere, but an invitation to one of the Careys' house-parties was still highly-prized. Visitors from Europe and even as far away as the United States would often disembark at the railway-halt some miles distant or come sliding up the country lanes in their Hispano-Suizas or Mercedes-Benzes. The presence of Rowena's sisters and their society friends, and of Hugh's industrial and political acquaintances, kept the house in a state of constant activity. And most weekends the lawns beyond the terrace, the tennis courts, and the drawing room, echoed to youthful, careless laughter; while, in the library, graver voices exchanged opinions on the increasingly baleful state of the world and the war that was certainly coming.

And then the war came.

But, despite the rigours of Invasion and Occupation, Winscombe Court kept its reputation: it still had a name for its busy social life, for its hospitality, and for the discreet conversation of powerful men.

At least, it had until recently. At Winscombe, as elsewhere, there had been some drastic changes in the last months. And, among other things, it was these changes which occupied Simon Carey, as, with his shotgun under his arm, he made his morning circuit of the grounds.

Jolly drastic! he thought, as he walked up from the water-meadows. After all, his father's factories had all been closed, the staff at the Court had been dismissed and parts of the house had been shut up, and without any warning he had been taken away from school. And there were, he knew, even greater changes in the offing. But those he was prepared for. Those were changes he was looking forward to.

Simon completed his rounds, returned to the house, and, having locked his gun away, popped into the kitchen to see what Mrs Cato, the housekeeper, was preparing for lunch.

Mrs Cato was the only remaining member of the Careys' staff. There had never been any question of dismissing Mrs Cato. She had been with Miss Rowena since she was a girl.

The housekeeper looked up from the sink where she was washing her hands. 'There you are, Mr Simon,' she said, reaching for the towel; 'you haven't forgotten that your father wants to see you in the library, have you?'

'Any idea what it's about, Mrs Cato?'

'No, I haven't,' she replied. 'But Madam and Miss Felicity have also been summoned.'

'Have they? I say!' he said with surprise, as she followed him out. 'Are you coming too?'

'I am.'

'It must be good news, then—don't you think?'

But Mrs Cato did not reply.

Frank was home again.

He was standing at the gate outside the cottage in Shevington. Nan Tate's cottage. He was looking down the lane. And, almost at once, a figure appeared hurrying up from the village: a figure in an old raincoat, the raincoat that Frank knew smelt of machine-oil, just as surely as he knew that the haversack over the man's shoulder contained a sandwich tin in which there'd be half a sandwich which had been saved for him. The figure saw him and started to wave. 'Frank?' he called. 'Frank, I hoped I'd find you here, old son. Sorry, I've been so long.' 'Dad?' he called, starting down the lane towards him. 'Dad!' And his dad broke into a run . . .

35

But he never reached him.

Frank rubbed his eyes. He was in that strange room still, the one with the empty spaces on the walls and the shutters at the window. And that girl—Felicity, that was her name—she was there, next to the bed.

'You've been tossing and turning,' she said. 'You won't get better if you don't sleep properly, you know.'

'I was dreaming,' he said. It was The Dream—the same one he used to have so often in the months after his dad disappeared. He hadn't dreamt that dream for ages.

'Listen,' he said, 'you know what you said the other day about the White Horse . . . you know, that you could see it from here?'

'You can.'

'Is the White Horse anywhere near Charborough?'

'Why do you want to know that?'

'No particular reason. Is it?'

But she didn't answer. Instead, she began turning the pages of her book.

'You're always reading that book,' he said.

'I find it reassuring,' she said. 'It's Tennyson. It's *The Idylls of the King*.'

'What're idylls?'

'They're stories. Poetry stories about King Arthur and his Knights. Arthur and Queen Guinevere and Sir Lancelot; and Merlin, of course, he was their magician.'

'Is it good?'

'It's sad. But there are lots of fine things as well. People behaving bravely and being generous and noble. It's the way life should be, don't you think?'

'I suppose so.'

'Nanny Gale thought so. This was her book. She was given it when she was a little girl. She gave it to me to keep when she was . . . when she was sent away.'

'Why was she sent away?'

'She had the wrong opinions.'

'What, you mean, like a Nazi? Was she a Nazi?'

'Oh, no! No, she was a very kind person. She was the

kindest person I've ever known. She loved this book. She used to read it to me when I was very small. It's the way she said the world should be. But it isn't, is it?'

'Things will get better,' he said. 'It's all going to change.'

She shook her head. 'People always promise you that,' she said. 'They always say things are going to get better; that everything's going to be perfectly wonderful. And you want to believe them. But that isn't what happens. People insist everything is going to turn out for the best. Even father does. But . . .' she hesitated, 'I don't think it is, Eric.'

'You mustn't think like that.'

'That's what father says. He says I have to be cheerful.'

'He's right. If we give up they could beat us even now.'

'Who?'

'The Jerries. The Jerries could still win if we give up.'

'What do you mean?'

'You never know with the Jerries, do you? Especially fighting on their own soil. They're bound to put up a fight. They might win.'

'Oh, but, Eric, they will. They always do.'

'No, they won't! Of course they won't! They're on the run. Don't give up. Consider Garibaldi!'

'Garibaldi?'

'That's what my nan used to say: "Consider Garibaldi!" Garibaldi kept on fighting whatever happened. Felicity?' She had got up and was making for the door. 'Felicity?' he called. 'What's the matter?'

'Please don't say anything else, Eric. You must stay in bed and rest. Because you must get better quickly. You have to be better before they come to take us.'

'Take you where?'

'I'm not allowed to tell you that,' she said. 'I have to go. Father has something important to tell us.'

And he heard the key turn in the lock.

A wintry sun shone wanly through the stained-glass of the drawing room window.

37

Hugh Carey stood with his back to the empty hearth. His wife sat opposite in one of the big leather armchairs. Simon and Felicity Winfred sat at the oak table, and Mrs Cato, her hands folded in front of her, stood beside them.

'These last months,' Hugh began gravely, 'these last months have not been an easy time for us. They have presented us with a considerable challenge. But it is a challenge to which we have risen. And we have survived. We have survived because, more than anything else . . . '

'We're going to win, father.'

'Yes, Simon, we are. Mrs Cato, wouldn't you feel more comfortable sitting down?'

'No, sir, thank you all the same.'

'Very well.' Hugh looked round the table thoughtfully. 'We have survived, above all,' he said, 'because we have remained true to our colours. It saddens me to recall how, when things became difficult, so many of our friends, friends who have sat at this very table, scuttled over to the other side as fast as their legs would carry them. Well, that isn't our way. That isn't the Carey way. We have held our ground. We have no regrets on that score.'

'None at all,' said Rowena Carey.

'Thank you, my dear. From the beginning, long before it was acceptable or fashionable to do so, we were among the few . . . '

'Felicity?' Mrs Carey tapped irritably on the arm of her chair.

'Yes, mother?'

'Can what you have there be in any way more important than what your father has to say?'

'Rowena . . . '

'One moment, Hugh. Well? Show me.' Mrs Carey took the book from her daughter. 'Tennyson?' she said.

'Yes.'

'Is this really the moment for medieval whimsy?'

'It isn't whimsy, mother . . . it's noble and good.'

'Oh, for goodness' sake, Felicity!' snapped her brother. 'Grow up!'

Mrs Carey closed the book and handed it back to her daughter. 'Please have the courtesy to pay attention while your father is speaking.'

'Yes, mother. I'm sorry, Daddy.'

'That's all right, darling. As a matter of fact, I haven't a great deal more to say. I simply wanted to assure you all that we have not been forgotten. I can tell you that without fear of contradiction. It is only a question of patience, and, of course, of remaining alert.'

'Let them do their worst, eh, father?'

'We must hope it doesn't come to that, Simon.' Hugh turned to Mrs Cato. 'Mrs Cato,' he said, 'would you care to say something?'

'May I, sir?'

'Please do.'

'Thank you, sir.' The housekeeper turned and smiled affectionately at her mistress and the children. 'Madam,' she said, 'Master Simon and Miss Felicity—what can I say other than to echo Mister Hugh's sentiments and endorse them wholeheartedly?'

'There are very few as loyal as you, Mrs Cato.'

'Thank you, madam. And if ever there was a time for loyalty I believe that time is now. Now's the time we shall see the wheat sorted from the chaff. Yes! And the chaff cast into the flames. This is the moment we've been waiting for. I've waited for twenty years. I've waited and watched the cause of National Socialism grow from a handful of vilified men and women into the greatest political and military force the world has ever known. Twenty glorious years in which one man has transformed his country from a decaying and moribund civilization into a proud and victorious one. My faith in Adolf Hitler is absolute. It can't be shaken by temporary reverses. I'm not that sort of woman.'

'We have never doubted you, Mrs Cato.'

'Thank you, sir. I am certain that the Leader is shaping our destiny today with the same determination and genius with which he has always directed his people. The outcome is not in doubt.' She raised her right arm. 'To victory,' she said. '*Sieg heil!*'

'To victory!' Hugh replied.

'You are a lesson to us all, Mrs Cato.'

'Thank you, madam.'

'*Sieg heil!*' said Simon. 'Absolutely!'

Chapter 5

It was, Les decided, like the time he'd been shot in the leg.

Someone had told him then that before he reached safety he must have walked three miles on that leg. The pain must have been terrific but he hadn't felt a thing. But afterwards it had really hurt. Like now. What had happened on the hillside two nights ago hurt far more now. Not the burns on his hand. They hurt, of course. But it was the other thing that hurt most. The thing that was losing the only friend he had. That hurt all the time.

He pulled on his trench coat and took down his cap. Keep moving, that was the answer. It was always the answer. Deliver leaflets for the Gifford's Mill lot? Play the errand boy? Why not? What did it matter? What did any of it matter any more? What had he got to lose?

The man beside the printing-press looked up as Les came in.

'Good lad,' he said. 'They're all ready for you. You're to take them to the chemist's shop in the square. Palmer's it's called. Just follow the road into town, you can't miss it. Tell Mr Palmer it's the painkillers he was expecting.'

'Can't I just hand them out?'

'No. We've got our ways of doing things. People have been sitting up and taking notice since that train wreck. Everyone wants to fight back now.'

'Did your lot do that?'

'The train? No, that was the partisans. Mind you, I think that sort of thing can be counter-productive. Uncovering the White Horse, now—that was a stroke of genius! Good

41

propaganda. That sort of thing can achieve more than all the explosions and suchlike.'

'Is that right?' said Les. It was clear which method Les preferred.

'Now, listen, nothing reckless,' said the printer. 'You're to take no risks. Just deliver the leaflets and get back here in one piece. Have a read of one as you go.'

'No, thanks,' said Les. 'I don't need nobody to tell me who the enemy is.'

It took him only ten minutes to reach the square and no time at all to spot Palmer's the chemist's. But what interested Les more, much more, was the church which overlooked the square. Especially its tower.

He sat down casually on a bench opposite the church-yard.

The main doors were locked and sealed, he could see that. But the narrow door at the foot of the tower was secured by a simple padlock. They might as well have left it wide open.

What had the printer said? 'We've got our ways of doing things'? Well, so have I, pal! He'd show these yokels how it was done! He could distribute more leaflets in five minutes than they could in an entire day.

It was dark inside. The windows were grimed and there was dust, damp, and bird droppings everywhere, but he easily found the narrow stairs. When he reached the hatch at the top he pulled back the rusted bolt and opened it carefully. Outside, the windswept sky was streaming by. It was perfect. He propped the hatch open with some fallen masonry and made his way to the parapet. He was amazed how small people looked. And, more importantly, how none of them ever seemed to look up.

Now he'd show them. He pulled a fistful of leaflets from the parcel, leaned forward, and threw them into the air. The leaflets lifted, spread themselves on the wind, and then began to drift down over the town like a flock of circling gulls.

And then he saw the car. It was cruising slowly on the other side of the square.

Coppers! And coming his way.

But if he was fast, really fast, he could be down and out of the tower before they realized where the leaflets were coming from.

Les hurled himself through the hatch and down the stairs. When he stepped out breathlessly into the church-yard some of the leaflets had already reached the ground. They lay scattered among the gravestones like fallen blossom.

He didn't even see the heavy fist that knocked him to the ground.

The policemen dragged him to the car and threw him onto the back seat. The one who slid in beside him was in plain clothes. He pulled the remaining leaflets from Les's pocket, and then, searching the other pocket, found the pistol concealed there. 'Well, well,' he said, 'looks like we've got ourselves a proper desperado.'

Les wiped the blood from his nose with the back of his hand. His head was still swimming from the blow. 'Go to 'ell!' he muttered.

'You bloody terrorist!' said the policeman and punched him again savagely. 'That's where you're going to wish you were after half an hour with me.'

The car drove only a few hundred yards, into a street just off the square. There it turned down an alley, which led to a high-walled yard at the back of the police station. Les was hustled across the yard and up some dark stairs to a windowless room on the first floor. The door was slammed shut and he was pushed down onto a chair in front of a large table. The table was the only thing in the room. And the only thing on the table was a policeman's truncheon.

His colleague took up a position somewhere behind Les and the plain-clothes policeman sat down on the edge of the table.

'All I want is names,' he said. 'All right? Tell me now and you'll save yourself a lot of pain.'

Les said nothing.

The policeman smiled at his colleague. 'Know what,' he said, 'I think we've got ourselves another Greta Garbo.' He reached forward and tapped Les on the knee confidentially. 'Sonny,' he said, 'I've had more silent heroes in here than you've had hot dinners. Now you just be a good boy and tell me where you got those leaflets? Eh? Who gave—' He was interrupted by a knock at the door and shouted angrily: 'Not now!'

But the door opened none the less and a constable came in. 'It's urgent, Commander,' he said. 'They want you down in the yard.' He leaned forward and whispered something in the policeman's ear. At which the policeman got up and, beckoning to his companion, followed the constable out.

Les heard the door close. He shook his head, trying desperately to collect his thoughts. And looked up. And couldn't believe his eyes. The room was empty. He shook his head again. The room was empty. They'd gone. They'd left him. They had. He stumbled out of the chair. And stood swaying in front of the table. There was only the one door—the door they'd brought him in by—the door they'd just gone through. No! There—behind him! There was another. He stumbled across and put his ear to the second door. Silence. He opened it carefully and looked out. The corridor was empty. There were stairs at one end. He staggered to the top of the stairs and started down, supporting himself against the wall. At the bottom of the stairs was a reception area and beyond that were the doors to the street.

The uniformed sergeant behind the counter looked up.

'Where d'you think you're going to?' he said.

'I'm . . . I've . . . I've had a nose-bleed,' said Les quickly. And held out his bloodstained fingers. 'See? I . . . I came to give information and my nose started to bleed.'

'I never saw you come in,' said the sergeant.

'In the back way,' said Les. 'I came in the back way. Confidential. You know, so's not to be seen.'

'Oh, right.'

'And the . . . the man upstairs . . . '

'Commander Harris?'

'He said I should get the bleeding seen to. Cos I wasn't no use to him the state I'm in.'

'I can see that. You'd better try Palmer's, the chemist's. He'll sort you out.'

As the sergeant spoke there were two pistol-shots from the rear of the building.

'And don't be long,' he said. 'The Commander don't like being kept waiting.'

Les tried to hurry. But his head was spinning and his legs felt weak. He hadn't gone more than twenty yards when he heard the shouts. He looked back and saw the Commander and his colleague standing on the steps of the police station. The sergeant was with them and was pointing in the other direction, towards the square. Les gathered himself. He had to run. There was nothing else for it.

'Hat!' The young woman scooped his cap from his head. 'Now the raincoat!' she said. 'Quickly! Take it off and sling it over your shoulder.' And with that she hauled him across the pavement and in through a pair of heavy ornamental doors.

The pale-faced girl sitting in the glass-fronted ticket-office looked up from the magazine she was reading. 'Was it *Death by Firelight* you were hoping for?' she asked.

'That'll do,' said the young woman. 'Two in the stalls for tonight.'

'I'm ever so sorry. There's no performance tonight.'

'Or any other night,' observed the man in the pork-pie hat who emerged from the curtained doorway nearby. 'I'm afraid we've had to cancel. First time in thirty years. Unpardonable but there was no alternative.'

He was interrupted by a shout from the street and the main doors were thrown open. 'Any of you seen a lad?' a voice called. 'Cap and raincoat and a bloody nose?'

Les felt the young woman's fingers tighten on his arm. And saw her other hand slip into her pocket. They had their backs to the policeman but he would only have to come a step or two further in and he was bound to see Les's bloodstained face.

The man in the pork-pie hat strode across to the door. 'Dear me,' he said with great concern. 'He sounds a desperate sort, officer. No—I'm delighted to say we've seen no sign of him at all.'

The policeman swore, pushed back through the doors, and disappeared along the street.

The man took off his hat and fanned himself vigorously. 'Turned rather humid, don't you think?' he said.

The young woman smiled. 'Thank you.'

'Happy to be of service,' he said. He took out a large, brightly-coloured handkerchief and handed it to Les. 'You'd better tidy yourself up. I'm told spittle's a first-class antiseptic.' Then he turned to the girl in the ticket-office: 'Been busy, Doreen?'

'There's been a lot of interest, Mr Selwyn,' she said. 'And disappointment, of course.'

'Of course. It's unpardonable! To up sticks without so much as "Goodnight, sweet prince!" I should have trusted my instincts, Doreen. I always felt Connors was a wrong 'un!'

'It does seem odd, doesn't it, Mr Selwyn?'

'Rum, Doreen—very rum!'

'And such a nice-looking young man.'

'Handsome is, Doreen, as handsome does!'

'Thanks, mister,' said Les, handing back the handkerchief.

'You're more than welcome.'

Les turned to the young woman. 'And thank you and all.'

She was in her early twenties with a fresh complexion and dark brown hair tucked up into a bun. 'Don't thank me yet,' she said. 'We've still got to get out of here.'

'If it's a discreet exit you're looking for I suggest you go through the curtain,' said the man in the pork-pie hat, and indicated the door from which he had emerged. 'The corridor on the other side leads to the stage door. Good luck

46

to you.' He turned back to the girl in the box office. 'I've been thinking, Doreen!' he said. 'Do you recall, *One Moment of Madness*? Simple froth but rather cheering. And it would require only the five of us. We could rehearse it this afternoon and have it ready for the matinée tomorrow . . . '

'I'll be all right now, miss,' said Les, once they were clear of the town. 'You'll get into bother if you're caught with me.'

'Oh, I don't intend getting into bother,' she said. 'With you or anyone else.' She seemed to know the streets and lanes like the back of her hand and it had taken them only ten minutes or so to reach the outskirts. They were standing at the edge of a field of allotments overlooking the railway line.

'You don't understand,' he said. 'I don't need help.'

'Don't you? So how come you ended up in the police station?'

Les didn't reply.

'You do know they're shooting people in that yard at the back, don't you?' she said matter-of-factly. 'You see, I saw you on the tower. I know it was you who threw the leaflets. That's worth a bullet as far as Commander Harris is concerned.'

'So what?'

'Just so you know. But I'm not going to stand here arguing. My advice is to swallow some of that pride and stay alive.'

She walked away between the rows of vegetables and he saw her knock at the door of one of the ramshackle huts. It was opened by an elderly man and she went inside. She reappeared almost at once with two bicycles.

'Well?' she called. 'Are you coming?'

He felt a bit of a fool. Riding a bike wasn't something he'd been prepared for. But he managed. And she didn't actually laugh at him. Besides, they were in too much of a hurry for conversation.

Once clear of the town they began the climb into the hills. They rode a long, high ridge for a quarter of an hour or so and then she turned them off down a narrow sheep-track which descended steeply to an abandoned quarry. Littered across the bottom of the quarry were pieces of rusting machinery, and against one side were three corrugated-metal sheds.

They dismounted for the last part of the descent, and, as they did so, two figures appeared. The smaller of the two, a bespectacled little man in a sleeveless leather jerkin, came to a halt, and waited with an irritable scowl on his face: the other, a tall, fair-haired young man in a faded RAF greatcoat, waved.

'All well, Gwen?' he called.

'All well, "Wings",' she replied. And she and Les wheeled their bicycles across to where the two men stood.

'Any problems?' said the other man.

'Not really,' she said.

'Who's this?'

'I don't know his name. We haven't had time for pleasantries.'

'The name's Gill,' said Les, 'Les Gill. Are you partisans?'

'He was distributing leaflets,' she said.

'One of the Gifford's Mill people?'

'Hardly. He was doing it from the top of the church tower. Not quite their style. Harris picked him up.'

'Then what the hell's he doing here?'

'He walked out.'

'He did what?'

'He walked out of the police station, as cool as you like.'

'Nobody walks out of that place, girl—not if Harris and his pals don't want them to.'

'Oh, come on, Mervyn! Look at him,' said the younger man. 'The poor blighter's taken a beating.'

'Leave this to me, "Wings". Give us your papers, boy.'

'Papers? I can't, can I? That copper's got them.'

'Oh, he has, has he? Isn't that convenient! For God's

sake, Gwen, why in the name of everything did you bring
this boy here?'

'What else was I supposed to do?' said the young woman.
'I could hardly leave him to their tender mercies.'

'Listen to me, girl . . . Dammit, he could be anybody.'

'What, a Jerry stooge, is that it?' said Les. 'Is that what
you're thinking?'

'Are you saying you're not?'

'I've spent the last two years killing Jerries not stooging
for 'em,' said Les angrily. He turned to the young
woman. 'Thanks for helping me,' he said. 'I owe you.' Then
he threw down the bike and started away back up the
hill.

'Wait!' She ran after him. 'Don't be stupid,' she said,
grabbing his sleeve. 'Come back. Come back and let me
see to that nose. Come on. I'm Gwen, by the way: Gwen
Wood.'

He didn't resist.

'You were a bit hard on him, Mervyn,' said 'Wings', as
they watched her lead Les across to the largest of the sheds.
'It must have taken plenty of pluck to walk out of that
place.'

'That's as maybe. But how better to plant someone on
us, eh? Harris and his crowd are Nazis, man. They didn't
go to public school. How often do I have to tell you?'

The inside of the shed was furnished with a table, a few
benches, and around the walls some makeshift beds assem-
bled from straw bales. There were one or two other rooms
leading off from the main area; and blackout material had
been rigged over the windows.

Gwen sat Les down at the table and opened up a battered
first-aid box. He winced as she wiped the blood from the
side of his nose.

'I don't think it's broken,' she said. 'It looks like Harris
fetched you a real pearler.'

'He took me by surprise,' said Les defensively.

'Of course he did. And what have you done to your
hand?'

49

Les shrugged. 'It got burnt,' he said. 'They put a bandage on it for me. At the Mill.'

'I'd better look at that too. You have been in the wars.'

'Listen, are you the partisans who did the train?'

She nodded.

'Is this all there is,' he said, 'just you three?'

'We've got volunteers and watchers all over the area. They go to earth except when we need them.'

There was a moan from the straw bales and Les looked round.

'It's all right,' she said. 'You're not our only guest.'

'Who is it?'

'He's called Bill. We found him wandering about the hills. He's had a tough time of it.'

The figure in the straw had pulled the blanket over his head but as he turned it fell away from his face. His hair had been cropped almost to his scalp, and his features were haggard and pale. His eyes remained shut but his arm reached up restlessly to brush something away. Then he pulled the covers over his head again and turned back to the wall.

'He was in one of the Nazis' camps,' said Gwen. 'There's always somebody worse off than yourself, eh, Les?'

Chapter 6

Rowena Carey looked up from her book as her husband came into the drawing room. 'Is there any word, Hugh?'

'None,' he said, and slumped down into an armchair. 'I've been waiting by the phone all morning.'

'I daresay it will ring when you least expect it.'

'I do envy your composure, Rowena.'

'What's that, Hugh?'

'The situation isn't exactly favourable, you know. I've tried not to alarm the children but . . . '

'It's a lesson they have to learn, Hugh. They have to learn just how fragile civilization can be once real authority is withdrawn.'

Hugh Carey got up and began to pace backwards and forwards in front of the fireplace. 'At least there's been no sign of those roughs Simon saw down by the Lodge the other morning.'

'Riff-raff.'

'Possibly.'

'Are you suggesting they weren't riff-raff?'

'You know what I mean, Rowena. There are people out there who'd be only too happy to come swarming up that drive and take it out on us.'

'But that won't be allowed to happen, Hugh. We've been given assurances—you know that perfectly well. Ah! There, what did I say?'

The phone had begun to ring.

As Hugh was hurrying across the hall he met his daughter. She was wearing a cloak with a hood which she had

51

pulled up over her head; and she was carrying a small wicker basket with a cloth over it.

'Felicity?' he said. 'What are you doing?'

'I'm going to have a picnic,' she said. 'To cheer myself up.'

'Are you? What a good idea. Look, darling . . . ' The phone continued to ring insistently. 'I'm sorry, Felicity, I really have to see who that is,' he said. 'But, look here, you mustn't be sad, you know. It'll all be resolved soon.'

'Daddy . . . ?'

'And please don't go too far from the house. Yes?' she heard him say as he picked up the phone. 'Yes, speaking . . . Is that you? . . . At last!'

And then he saw her listening and closed the study door.

Supporting himself against the wall, Frank made his way slowly along the side of the room. There seemed to be more strength in his legs now. But by the time he reached the window he was dizzy with the effort.

He pulled gently at the shutters and they gave an inch or two. Not far below him was a cobbled stableyard. But a sound from Felicity's room made him close the shutters again quickly. Someone was moving about, shifting things. She was back. He thought for a moment of calling out to her but then he heard her voice. She was shouting.

'How ignoble! Oh, Simon, how ignoble!'

'Oh, do shut up,' a second voice replied. 'And look at you! Good Lord, who do you think you are, Red Riding Hood?'

Felicity Winfred Carey confronted her brother angrily from the doorway. 'How could you? How dare you! This is my room, Simon. It's mine.'

'Not when you fill it with secrets it isn't.'

'Secrets?'

'You know what I'm talking about. You're a bigger fool than I took you for if you really think you can go on hiding it from me, you know? Do you hear me, Felicity? I don't care how long it takes I'm going to find it.'

'Get out! Get out! Get out!'

'Or what?'

'Or I'll tell . . . '

'Who? Tell Nanny? That wretched Gale woman? She's gone, so you can't go whining to her.' And Simon grasped the handle of the nanny's old room and began to turn it. At once Felicity let out such a piercing scream, accompanied by repeated shouts of 'Get out! Get out! Get out!' that Simon Carey put his hands over his ears and backed away: 'All right, all right! There's no need to get hysterical!' he said. 'Dammit, Felicity, you haven't heard the last of this.' He hurried out and she slammed the door behind him.

Moments later Frank heard the key turn in his own door and she came in.

'What are you doing out of bed?' she demanded.

'I was just . . . you know.' He gestured towards the lavatory with his thumb.

'Oh,' she said, 'I'm sorry, I didn't mean to be rude.'

'Are you all right?' he said.

But she ignored his question. 'I've brought you some apples,' she said. She pulled the cloth from the basket and tipped the fruit onto the counterpane. 'Eat them up, they keep the doctor away.'

She sat down in her usual place and watched Frank as he ate hungrily.

'Eric,' she said after a while, 'would you mind if I spoke to you seriously?'

'If you like.'

'Eric, do you think one should be fond of one's family?'

'Fond of them?'

'Yes. It's a simple enough question.'

'I suppose so. I've only got my dad.'

'But you're fond of him?'

'I haven't seen him for four years.'

'Whyever not?'

'He was captured the night the Germans landed.'

'What happened to him?'

'I don't know. He sent a letter through the Red Cross saying he'd been put to work on building roads. That was a year after he was captured. He was alive then. I tried to go and look for him once but . . . '

'What?'

'Other things happened.'

'And what about your mother?'

'I don't remember her. She left us when I was small. She led Dad a bit of a dance. Or so my nan used to say.'

'I adore dancing.'

'Do you? I had a cousin who liked dancing. Her name was Rose.'

'Could she foxtrot? I'd almost mastered the foxtrot when all this started. No one comes to dance here any more. It's this horrible war. Oh, I hate it so much!' She looked at him expectantly. 'I'm sorry, I know one isn't supposed to say things like that.'

'Why not?' he said.

'Because.'

'But it is,' he said; 'the war is horrible.'

'Do you think so? Oh, Eric, I'm so glad you do!' she said excitedly. 'It is, isn't it! So horrible. And life could be so . . . If you read this book you'd know what I mean. The people in this book . . . I mean, I know they're not real but they live such noble lives. They do fine things, or at least they try to. I think that's important, don't you? Trying to do fine things? Far more important than . . . well, all the rest of it: all the other stories they tell you. All the things people tell you are true and important. Have you any brothers and sisters?'

'An auntie and some cousins. And my grandmother— but she died.'

'I have a brother,' she said. 'He's a brute. His name's . . . well, you don't need to know his name. He hates me.'

'Why?'

'That's the sort of person he is. He hasn't any proper friends. He hates everyone. There are lots of people like that, aren't there? But you don't hate everyone, do you?'

'Not especially.'

She took a deep breath and seemed to be considering carefully what to say next. 'Eric,' she said, 'did you have a merry Christmas?'

'How do you mean?'

'Ours was rather forlorn. We had so few cards. Hardly enough to cover the mantelpiece. But we did have chicken for lunch. Are you fond of chicken?'

'Chicken?' he said. 'Yes, I think so.'

'Good. Then you understand all about wishbones.'

'What, you mean pulling them and making a wish?'

'That's right. Eric, you must swear never to tell anyone what I'm going to tell you. Never. Do you swear?'

'If you want me to.'

'The fact is,' she said, and drew her chair closer to the bed; 'the fact is, I've still got it.'

'Got what?'

'The wishbone. When Mrs Cato, she's our housekeeper, left the carcass in the kitchen I crept in and took it.'

'Why?'

'To keep it safe. I'm saving it, you see, until there's a really important wish to make. One that's a matter of life and death. There will be one,' she said, 'I'm sure there will.'

'But aren't you supposed to have somebody to pull it with?'

'Oh, no,' she said. 'Simon mustn't have any part of it. That's why I've hidden it.'

'Who's Simon?'

'My brother. That was him just now. Shouting. He'll cheat and pull really hard and win, you see. And then he'll wish for something horrible. That's why he desperately wants to find it. But now that you're here, Eric . . . even if it's only for a little while . . . I think things are going to be all right.' She smiled. 'I've got to go now but I'll be back later. Keep still. And be very quiet.'

What an odd girl she was! She didn't seem quite right in the head, poor kid.

55

Frank slid out of bed and made his way across to the window. Yes, there was definitely more strength in his legs! A lot more. He eased open the shutters. Just an inch or two. From the window it was four or five feet to the roof of the outhouse. And from there he could easily scramble down into the yard. From there . . . Well, from there it was only a question of finding the road. And then a day's tramp . . . maybe less . . . to Charborough and Gifford's Mill. That's where Les would have headed.

Finding that damned wishbone had become a matter of principle. Felicity couldn't be allowed to get away with it. She got away with quite enough as it was. In the month and more since Christmas Simon Carey had searched every imaginable hiding-place. It certainly wasn't the first time he'd searched her room. And it wouldn't be the last no matter how much she screamed and carried on. But all his searches had been fruitless. Which was why, this morning, he had decided on a new strategy. And Simon had a feeling that this morning things would be different.

He slipped across the hall and through the door to the East Wing, closing it quietly behind him.

This morning he was going to start looking in the parts of the house which had been closed up: the rooms where the guests used to stay. He was the first to admit that it was a considerable undertaking. But he wouldn't have to search every room, would he? Because there were bound to be tell-tale signs where anyone had been recently, wouldn't there? Of course, there would. That would be the giveaway.

He was halfway up the stairs when he saw it. Clear as day, there on the banister: a long smear in the dust as though someone's sleeve had brushed past. 'Oh, Simon Carey!' he exclaimed. 'You jammy type! And you've only just begun! Oh, Felicity, you really are so completely inept!'

He stood very still and listened. Good Lord—she was up there! She was up there in one of the rooms on the floor above! He put his hand over his mouth to stop himself laughing. Then he tiptoed stealthily to the top of the stairs and along the carpeted corridor. He took a deep breath. 'Well, well,' he said, throwing open the door. 'Look what I've found.'

His mother looked up at him. 'Simon, dear,' she said, 'what is it?'

'Mother? I thought . . . '

'What do you want?'

'I heard something and . . . '

'You shouldn't be in this part of the house, darling.'

Mrs Cato was there too. She was smoothing out the freshly-laundered sheet which had been laid on the bed. The dust-covers had been removed from the furniture and the windows were open. 'Mother, what are you doing?' he asked.

'It couldn't possibly be of any interest to you, Simon. Off you go. This minute, please. Mrs Cato and I are fearfully busy.'

'Is someone coming to stay?'

'Darling, please! Go away.'

'All right, I'm going!' he said sullenly. But he took one last look as he went out. They'd even laid a fire in the grate.

He collected his waterproof from the hook by the back door and walked round into the stableyard.

His mother had treated him like a child. And in front of Mrs Cato. Well, he wasn't a child. Damn bloody Felicity! It was her behaviour made people treat them like children. She really was beyond the pale. Mad as a bally hatter half the time. She was getting more and more like that awful girl in the play they'd put on at school last term. *Hamlet*. That was the one. There was a mad girl in that who traipsed about the place with dead flowers and I don't know what else. His idiot sister wasn't far short of that. She was a disgrace. Well, that was all going to change. Everything was going to be a lot different . . . quite soon. Soon he'd be in a situation where he'd be appreciated.

He stood in the shelter of the stables looking up at the

57

falling rain and feeling very sorry for himself. The morning, which had seemed so full of promise, was turning out rather badly.

Which was when he saw the shutters move. Or, at least, he thought he did. Because they shouldn't have. The shutters on that side of the house had all been secured weeks ago. But those two had moved. He was sure they had. He drew back against the wall and watched. And saw them move again . . . only an inch or two but they definitely moved. Which room was it? He counted the windows. And counted them again. But that was Nanny Gale's old room. That room hadn't been used since that awful woman and her opinions had been sent packing and . . . 'Oh, you bally oaf!' he exclaimed. 'Oh, you bally bally oaf! Oh, I say! Got you, my girl! Got you!'

She was coming downstairs as he burst in from the yard. He put on his best smile.

'Hello, Felicity,' he said.

She stopped not far from the bottom of the stairs. 'Why are you smiling like that?' she said.

'Oh, I just feel like smiling. It's such a wonderful morning. And I've been thinking. Look here, don't you think this wishbone business has gone far enough?'

She was on her guard at once. 'No!' she said. 'No, I don't.'

'But don't you think it's all rather silly?'

'Oh, no! You won't get me to tell you like that, Simon.'

'Whatever can you mean?'

'Because I don't think it is silly, as a matter of fact.'

'Felicity, I wasn't trying to get you to tell me. Honestly. Cross my heart.'

'Yes, you were.'

'But I don't want you to tell me, I swear.'

'Why not?' she said suspiciously.

He grinned. 'Because, dear girl, I don't need you to.'

'What do you mean?'

'Because I know. I know where the wishbone is.'

'But you . . . No, you don't!'

He laughed. 'Oh, your face is such a picture!' he said. 'You look utterly crestfallen. Well? Shall we go and get it? We'll pull it together, shall we?'

He pushed her aside and started up the stairs. She watched in amazement for a moment and then ran after him. 'Simon?' she said, clinging to his arm. 'Where are you going? Simon, it's not fair!'

'You shouldn't have secrets, Felicity. It isn't healthy.'

When they reached the landing she ran round in front of him and barred his way. 'You shan't!' she said defiantly. 'You shan't. It's mine. And you don't know where it is! You don't!'

'Yes, I do.'

'You don't! You don't! Where is it, then?'

'Did you really think you could hide it? From me? Did you?' He brushed past her and ran on, taking the stairs two at a time with his sister stumbling after him.

'Simon!' she pleaded. 'Simon, wait!'

He pushed open her door and crossed quickly to the other side of the room. 'Locked?' he said, rattling the handle of Nanny Gale's room. 'Where's the key, Felicity? You'd better tell me, you know.'

'No, Simon, please! The wishbone's not there, Simon— I swear. Please, please go away. I'll show you where it really is, I promise. You can have the wretched wishbone. I don't care about it any more.'

'What do you mean? You do care about it, I know you do.' And a terrible suspicion came into his head. 'Dammit, Felicity,' he said, 'you haven't made the wish already, have you? Have you? You've pulled it already, haven't you?' He grabbed her wrist and began to twist it painfully. 'You have, haven't you? That'd be just like you.'

'Simon, don't!' she shouted. 'I haven't!'

'Then where's the key to this door?'

'I don't know.'

But he saw her desperate glance to the lintel above. 'Pathetic!' he said, reaching up. 'And now we'll put a stop to this childishness.'

'Simon, please!'

He slipped the key into the lock, turned it, and threw open the door.

'Good heavens!' he said. 'Who the devil are you?'

Chapter 7

Hugh Carey smiled. 'Well, Eric,' he said, 'this must all have been rather disconcerting for you.'

'I wish I'd been there,' said Simon.

'Don't be crass, Simon,' said Mrs Carey. 'There's nothing very enviable about having bombs dropped on you. Are you in any pain, Eric?'

'No,' said Frank. 'Just headaches now and then. It's getting better.'

'I'm glad to hear it. But one can never be too careful. The consequences of something like this could be very disagreeable. Don't you agree, Hugh?'

'Very disagreeable,' said her husband. 'By the way, Eric, I must apologize for my daughter's extraordinary behaviour.'

'She didn't mean any harm,' said Frank. 'She said . . . '

Mr Carey laughed. 'She probably said all sorts. I'm afraid you mustn't believe everything my daughter tells you.'

'Anything she tells you,' said Simon.

Mrs Carey smiled. 'Felicity can be rather fanciful.'

'She was doing her best,' said Frank.

'Well, it's very decent of you to see it like that. But now you must let us do our best to make up for what's happened. What do you think, Hugh?'

'Yes, indeed, my dear. And the first thing to do is get you out of those rags and spruce you up a bit, young man.'

'The thing is,' said Frank, 'I ought to be getting on . . . '

'All in good time, eh?'

'We're placing Eric in your charge, Simon,' said Mrs Carey. 'You will make quite sure he's properly looked after, won't you?'

'Of course, mother.'

'And, Simon?' said Mr Carey.

'Father?'

'Well done.'

The boys went out and Hugh Carey got up from the table. 'What does that girl think she's playing at?' he said angrily. 'And at a time like this? God knows what sort of a pickle we'd be in if it hadn't been for Simon's vigilance.'

'We can't allow him to leave, Hugh.'

'What do you mean?'

'Not in the circumstances. Who knows what he's already seen and heard?'

'But he's been locked in that room.'

'For heaven's sake, Hugh—there's no knowing what Felicity may have told him.'

'But she doesn't know anything, Rowena. Not in any detail.'

'Details wouldn't be necessary. A hint would be more than enough if it reached the right quarters. And if matters were to miscarry we'd be held responsible. Remember that. We would pay the price.'

'You're right, of course. He'll have to stay until we . . . well, until the time comes. Simon will keep an eye on him.'

'A close eye. Now, if you'll excuse me, Hugh, there really is a great deal to do.'

Crouched on the landing above, Felicity Winfred Carey watched from between the banisters as her brother and Eric came out of the drawing room. Simon had triumphed yet again. He had taken Eric away from her the way he always took things away from her. Just like he'd taken Nanny Gale away from her. Telling father and mother what she'd said about the war so that mother wouldn't have her in the house and father had had to dismiss her. That's what Simon always did. But perhaps now he'd be satisfied. Perhaps now he'd give up looking for the wishbone. That, at least, would still be hers.

The two boys looked up and saw her watching them.

'You mustn't take too much notice of my sister,' said

Simon. 'She'll have lost interest in you already. She's a bit unhinged, you see. It's the war. Girls just aren't up to things like wars. It's not their forte. Mother's an exception, of course. But Felicity . . . it's got her down, d'you see? It's what they call "her nerves". She takes things to heart. Girls do, don't they?'

'I suppose so,' said Frank.

'I daresay you're a bit unhinged yourself. Being blown up and all. Now then—togs! We must get you out of those awful rags and into something decent. I've lots you can choose from. Let me give you a hand, Eric.'

And Simon Carey took Frank's arm and helped him slowly up the stairs.

'What do you mean you don't know?'

'I can't remember.'

'Start again!' Mervyn leaned forward across the table. 'From when the car stopped in the yard and they took you upstairs.'

'The one in charge . . . '

'Harris?'

'Harris—yes, that's what the copper at the desk called him.'

'Just the one copper at the desk, was there?'

'Yes. I think so. It's hard to remember. Harris had knocked me about, hadn't he!'

'They sat you down in the room.'

'Yes.'

'The room without the windows. Show me.' Mervyn pushed a pencilled plan of the police station towards Les. 'Show me again!'

'Mervyn, we know all this.'

'Details, "Wings"! Details, man! That's how we stay alive. Look at it!' Mervyn pointed to the plan. 'It's a death-trap! Harris could corner us in any one of those corridors.'

'There's always a risk,' said Gwen calmly; 'we know that. What do you say, "Wings"?'

'Piece of cake, Queen of my Heart,' said the airman and grinned.

'It's no such bloody thing!' snapped Mervyn. 'I won't be responsible for a risk on this scale.'

'We've got Harris and his men bottled up,' said Gwen. 'They're scared to venture out beyond the town. If we can put them out of action the whole county will get a fillip. What we need is another coup. Like the train. Like the White Horse.'

'And you've got me to help you this time,' said Les.

'Mervyn, we can't wait for the chief to get back. We don't know when that might be.'

'Scramble the flight, Mervyn. Let's have a crack at the blighters.'

'For goodness' sake! What sort of suicidal nonsense is that? Do you ever listen to yourself, "Wings"? Do you? I sometimes wonder what world you live in, man! It's not a damned fairy-story! I'm responsible for lives . . . '

'Stop it! Stop it, both of you,' said Gwen. 'Mervyn, will you sanction the attack? Well?'

Mervyn sighed. 'I don't like it. But it's necessary. Very well.'

'When do we start?' said Les enthusiastically.

'Oh, no. Not you.' Mervyn gathered up the plans.

'But you'll need all the—'

'Not you. You'll stay here.'

'That's not fair!'

'No arguments.'

'Come on, Les,' said Gwen.

Les followed her out of the shed and up onto the slope overlooking the valley. 'What's he got against me?' he said angrily. 'What does he think I'm going to do?'

'Mervyn's a very careful man,' she said. 'We've lost good comrades to Commander Harris and his pals. And Mervyn's . . . well, Mervyn takes these things very seriously.'

'Don't you?'

'Yes. But it's different for Mervyn. He was in Spain, you see. During the Civil War. He fought against the fascists there. Mervyn's been fighting them a long time. That's why he's here. That's why he's in command while the chief's away.'

'You mean he ain't your proper chief?'

'The chief's at a meeting of resistance leaders. It's all very hush-hush. So—what about you?'

'What about me, what?'

'Why are you here?'

'I don't like Germans.'

'They're not all Germans, Les. Harris and his men are as English as they come. We shouldn't kid ourselves. There are plenty of people who decided they had more in common with the Jerries than their own countrymen. The Nazis didn't have to go far when they went looking for friends. How's the hand feeling?'

'Better.'

'Good. You didn't tell me how you did it, did you?'

Les shrugged. 'I just did, that's all.'

'I see.' She took a deep breath. 'These hills are lovely, don't you think?' she said.

'Are you from round here?'

'No. Shropshire. We had a farm. My husband and I.'

'You married, then?'

'I was. He was killed.'

'Sorry.'

'You weren't to know. What about you?'

'I ain't married,' said Les hastily.

She laughed. 'What I meant was what about your family? Friends?'

'I had a friend,' he said. 'He got killed. And I had a sister but . . . ' Les shrugged.

'They've spoilt everything, haven't they,' she said, 'the Nazis? That's the one thing they're good at—spoiling things.'

'Gwen?' said Les. 'Listen, when you attack that police station . . . '

There was a shout from the yard below. And they turned to see 'Wings' striding up the hill towards them.

Gwen smiled. 'D'you know,' she said, 'I think "Wings" is the only one of us who really looks the part.'

'He looks like the ones I used to see on the newsreels at the pictures,' said Les. 'One of them Brylcreem boys in the Spitfires. All silk scarves and pound-note-ish!'

'He wasn't in Spitfires,' she said, 'he was in bombers. He was forced down and had to ditch in the sea not long before the surrender. The rest of his crew were drowned. Every one of them. And none of them much more than twenty years old. He was the only survivor.'

'I didn't know that.'

'No. That's why I'm telling you. You should never judge people too quickly, Les.' They watched the airman climbing up the hill towards them. 'He was very ill,' she said. 'In a hospital. For months on end. Then he found us.'

'You all right, young Les?' the airman enquired. 'Don't pay too much heed to Welsh Mervyn. His bark is distinctly worse than his bite. And his heart's in the right place.'

'I can handle him.'

'Course, you can. Good man. Gwen, could you come and look at the chap in the shed. He's coughing again.'

'See you later, Les.'

'Gwen?' Les called, as the two of them walked back down the hill. 'You'll make Mervyn take me with you, won't you?'

The young toff in the mirror looked back quizzically at Frank.

He hardly recognized himself. The men's hand-me-downs he had worn for the last two years had been replaced by a natty tweed jacket and grey flannel trousers, and both fitted pretty well.

'I must say you do look the part,' said Simon. 'But I'm not sure about that trilby.'

'It's my lucky hat,' said Frank.

'Eric, it's perfectly awful.'

'I've had it a long time.'

'Well, if you insist. Do choose some more things.' Simon

pointed to the pile of clothes which had been pulled from the drawers and thrown on the bed.

Frank shook his head. 'I can't take all those.'

'You might as well. I won't be able to take them with me.'

'Where are you going?'

'What?' Simon recovered himself quickly. 'Nowhere,' he said. 'Figure of speech, that's all. What I meant . . . Look here, you must forget I said that. You will, won't you? It's fearfully secret.'

'If you like.'

'Good fellow. Now, Eric, there must be something else you fancy?'

'The overcoat would be handy.'

'Take it!' Simon threw himself into a chair. 'So . . . what were you doing? You know, when the Yanks bombed you?'

Frank hesitated. 'Travelling,' he said.

'Really? Rather dangerous in times like these I would have thought. Move about a lot, do you?'

'A bit.'

'On your own?'

'Yes.'

'Been on your own long?'

'Since my dad . . . ' Frank shrugged.

'Oh, I see—dead is he?'

'No. He's with a Labour Unit. At least, I think he is.'

'Is he? Is he really?' Simon slapped the arm of the chair. 'Well done him! Father says you give a man back his dignity when you put him to work. I mean, if you take away a man's dignity there's no knowing what he'll put in its place, is there? It's the sort of thing father knows about. Father's had to close our factories, you see. Though they were all doing jolly well, as a matter of fact. But you know how it is these days. Listen, do you keep in touch with your father? You know, write to him and things?'

Frank frowned. Had Simon Carey any idea what a Forced Labour Unit was like? 'Well . . . you know,' he said.

'You don't mind me asking, do you?'

'No, course not. It's just . . . I don't know where he is.'

'Really? How irritating. Don't worry, it'll all be sorted out once the war's over. It won't be long now. Look, I daresay you could use a spot of fresh air after being locked up in my sister's dungeon? What about a turn on the roof?'

'The roof?'

'Yes. Come on, we'll go up through the attic.'

From the leads of Winscombe Court there was a long view down the valley. The hamlet of Winscombe lay tucked in the turn of the river and beyond that there were fields. And beyond that, in the far distance . . .

Felicity hadn't talked complete rubbish, after all. There it was. Even on a day like this, with scudding clouds and the promise of rain in the air, Frank could still make out the shape cut into the side of the distant hill.

'What's that?' he said. 'On the hill?'

'That's the White Horse,' said Simon. 'Some silliness the Ancient Brits put there more years ago than anyone can be bothered to remember. Anyone with any sense.'

'Which way is Charborough?'

'Why do you ask?'

'No special reason,' said Frank. 'It's just somewhere I've heard of.'

'Really? Can't think why. It's a dreadful hole. As a matter of fact it's not far from that awful old horse. Whoa!' A sudden gust of wind made them both stagger. Simon laughed. 'Listen,' he said, 'you'd better hold on to something. It can really blow across these tiles. I must say, Eric,' he resumed, making himself comfortable against one of the chimneys, 'it's a great relief to have another chap to talk to. I mean, father and I talk. He keeps me in the picture. And mother can go on for hours. Though I find some of it a bit hard to follow. And Mrs Cato's always good value. Of course, my sister's no earthly good at all when it comes to talking. Not sensibly. Not about important things. When I say important things what I mean to say is, you know, "the international situation". What's your reading of the way things stand? You know,' he said without waiting for an answer, 'what never ceases to astonish me is that old Tacitus knew it all all along. And Tacitus was writing . . . well, I don't know how many hundreds of years ago. And he was a Roman. You've read the *Germania* at school, I daresay? All that amazing stuff about the German tribes and how they kept themselves to themselves . . . Oh, I say . . . too late!'

Frank grabbed desperately for his hat but the sudden gust of wind had snatched it into the air and was carrying it out over the grounds below.

Simon laughed. Then: 'I say, what are you doing?' he said.

'I've got to get it back,' said Frank, turning towards the door through which they'd come.

'No, don't do that!' Simon's fingers closed around Frank's arm.

'But . . . '

'Better not! Fact is, Eric, it's not a good idea to go too far from the house. Don't get me wrong, it's perfectly safe as long as we stay put. Besides, you don't need that old hat any more. I'm sure I can find you something much more suitable.' He smiled and gestured courteously towards the iron ladder which dropped down to the attic door: 'Shall we?' he said.

Chapter 8

Shevington, West Sussex

It took three days for the Wehrmacht's engineers to decommission their Communications Headquarters at Shevington Hall.

What General von Schreier's men couldn't carry away with them they destroyed; piling the lawns and gardens with coils of cable, receivers, and transmitting equipment. Then they lit massive bonfires in front of the house and burned everything that could be burned: code-books, correspondence, and the mountainous files of four years of constant surveillance. It was these fires which brought about the rumour in Shevington that the Germans were going to burn down the Hall itself. And it was that rumour which, each morning, brought a dozen or so young men from the village to the woods above the Hall to watch the lorries loading up and hurrying east along the Middlebury Road.

But on the third day the Hall was still standing and it seemed that the threat had passed. As the last truck pulled away through the gates, Phil Gingell and four or five of the other lads lurking in the trees ran down through the Knot Garden and round to the lawn in front of the house. All that was left, abandoned at the foot of the main steps, was a grey Mercedes staff-car. The Germans had gone.

Nobody afterwards could remember who suggested it but someone said: 'Whatever else we do, we ought to pull down them perishin' flags!'

He was pointing to the two blood-red banners which

hung either side of the columned entrance, each with its swastika trapped in its white circle like a frantic spider.

'Dirty Nazi tripe!' said someone else.

And it was Phil Gingell who ran up the steps.

Just as General von Schreier and his secretary, Oberleutnant Werner Lang, together with the general's driver, came out of the building. When the driver saw the young man pulling at the flag he put down the suitcase he was carrying, took out his pistol and, despite the General's raised hand, pulled the trigger.

It was the last shot fired in anger in Shevington.

Rose Gingell slammed the saucepan down. The knives and forks on the draining-board rattled noisily.

What was the point of any of it? You could talk to 'em till you were blue in the face. You could explain things sensibly or you could rant and rave but none of it made a blind bit of difference. They never listened to a word you said to them. Husbands!

She looked up as her mother came hurrying in from the garden where she had been hanging out the washing.

'What's all the racket, girl? You'll wake our George.'

Rose glanced across at the pram which stood beside the fire.

'Oh, he's all right,' she said. 'Oh, ma—it's Phil.'

'He's gone up the Hall then?'

'The others called round for him. There's bound to be trouble. I've asked him time and time again not to go up there.'

'He'll be all right, girl.'

'They egg each other on, ma. What if the Germans was to arrest him? And take him away? What if we never saw him again?' Rose shook her head. 'Know what I been thinking?' she said. 'Oh, ma—what if he's just like our Frank?'

'Now don't say that, Rose.'

'That's what happened with Frank, wasn't it? When he

71

went off looking for his dad. He just walked out that door. And we never saw him again.'

Edith Worth sighed. 'I know,' she said. 'But there wasn't no way we could have stopped him. He had a mind of his own, Rose. Always did have. He was like your nan was Frank. What was it Nan used to say? "Consider Garibaldi!"'

Rose reached for the tea-towel and began to dry the plates. 'I think about him, you know,' she said. 'He was such a lovely kid. D'you ever think about him, ma?'

'Course I do,' said Edith wearily. She sat down in the old windsor chair by the range, her mother's old chair, Nan Tate's chair. She began to gently rock the pram in which her grandson was asleep. 'I think about Frank. And about his father, too. Me and my brother Bill wasn't ever the best of friends. We had our differences. Stubborn as each other, I daresay. But he was my brother. Ah, this war's done terrible things to us! There can't be a family anywhere it ain't caused pain and grief.'

'It's going to end, ma,' said Rose. 'And then things will be different.'

'Perhaps.'

'They will! That's what I keep telling Phil. I tell him it's all going to be different. And we've got to be ready for it. But it don't seem to make any difference. Men!'

'They've had the hope drained out of 'em, Rose. They've been left idle and helpless for so long.'

'And what are we women s'posed to have been doing, then? Sitting on our hands whistling "Dixie"? Oh, it makes me so angry.'

'It's different for the men, Rose.'

'Oh, is it? Is it really?' Rose dried her hands irritably.

'Course it is. They en't so . . . ' Edie got up suddenly. 'Is that you, Len?' she called.

Her husband came into the kitchen from the hall. He was pulling on his coat.

'D'you want a cup of tea, love?' she asked.

Len Worth shook his head. 'I've got things to do,' he said. Which was what he said every morning. Because every morning was the same: he got up not long before eleven o'clock, pulled on his coat and walked slowly down to Shevington Green where he and most of the other men from the village gossiped and grumbled away the hour or so before the Shevington Arms opened. Then they would adjourn to the public bar and spend the next couple of hours making their watery pint of beer last until it was time to go home to whatever their wives had managed to find to feed them on. Which generally wasn't much.

'I can brew one up in no time, eh?' said Edith. 'Me and Rose was going to have a cup . . . '

'Don't go on so, Edie! I told you . . . I've got things to do.'

Len pushed open the door and they heard his heavy footsteps on the cinder path.

'Things to do? Oh, yes? Down the Shevvy playing cock of the walk with his prisoner-of-war stories.' Rose shook her head. 'Oh, ma—what's happened to him?'

'Be fair, Rose. It's all he's got.'

'No, it en't!' Rose threw down the tea-towel. 'He's got promises to keep. He was so full of it when he got back from the prisoner-of-war camp. And after Nan Tate died. All the things he was going to do. And he never did repair that roof, did he? The damp in that back bedroom's getting worse and . . . '

There was a wail from the pram and Rose hurried over and lifted her baby out. 'It's all right, George,' she said gently; 'there now, George, it's all right.'

Edith smiled. 'Poor little chap, it's them teeth. You was a demon when your teeth come through, Rose. Your brother Colin, he was quieter altogether.' She stood up and stroked her grandson's head. 'It'll be all right, girl,' she said. 'You'll see. Phil's a sensible sort of chap. He won't be led on.'

'You damned butcher! You've killed him!'

General von Schreier's driver held his ground, his pistol

73

levelled at the group of young men shouting from the steps below.

But the General reached across and pushed the weapon aside. 'Enough,' he said.

'Herr General?'

'It is only a flag, Otto.'

The driver turned and looked at him in amazement. But the General was already moving off towards the waiting car.

From the back seat Von Schreier looked up at the grand country house that had been his home for the last four years. What a pleasure it had been to walk those elegant corridors, to inhabit its well-proportioned rooms—well, the ones those damned engineers hadn't stripped and filled with their wires and dials—and spend so many long and rewarding hours in its superb library. The General's mother had been an admirer of everything English and he had been brought up to appreciate such things.

Von Schreier turned to his secretary. He and Oberleutnant Werner Lang had been together since the triumphant days of 1940. The heady days of Warsaw, Amsterdam, Paris, and London. Of the inexorable advance. Of the inevitable victory.

'Tell me, Werner,' he said, 'do you think this could be construed as looting?' And he took a small sheet of paper from the pocket of his greatcoat.

'What is it, Herr General?'

'It was irresistible. It is from a folio I found in the library. Landscape sketches. Trees, as you see. And sheep. Eighteenth century. Do you think if I take this it will ensure that one day we will return to Shevington Hall?'

'All things are possible, Herr General.'

Von Schreier smiled. 'You're right, of course; I too think that it is most unlikely.' He glanced out of the window of the car. The young men had swarmed up the steps and were gathered round Phil Gingell. 'They will show us no mercy, Werner.'

'No, Herr General—none.'

The General straightened his shoulders. 'Why should they?' he said. 'We never showed any to them. Drive on, Otto.'

Vera Thrale had been gathering kindling near the edge of the wood when she heard the shot.

'Mildred?' she called to her companion. 'Trouble. That came from the direction of the Hall. Come along.'

And they set off at once.

The gamekeeper's wife and the young woman with her were no strangers to trouble. More often than not these days it was Vera Thrale and Mill to whom Shevington people turned whenever they were in difficulties. It was Vera who had convinced them that it was possible to survive; that they could keep starvation, an increasing possibility in those early months of 1945, at bay, if—and only if—they organized and pooled the produce they grew in their gardens. It was Vera, and her herbs and concoctions, who was called on more and more frequently whenever the doctor had no more medicines, or advice, available. It was Vera to whom everyone brought the increasingly numerous forms and demands required by the desperate Occupiers. There were one or two villagers, inevitably, who muttered about 'some people being too clever by half' but for the most part the tall, well-spoken woman with her colourful turbans and home-made clothing was welcomed wherever she went.

And with Vera went Mill. Mill Gill, the evacuee. When Mill and her brother Les had first come to the village they had been greeted with hostility and suspicion. Guttersnipes, was one of the more flattering things they'd been called. Mill was still known as the Cockney. But now it was said without rancour and with a grudging hint of acceptance.

Vera and Mill lived alone in Keeper's Cottage on the edge of the Shevington estate. And had done so ever since the day, two years before, when Alec Thrale had gone off

75

in search of Mill's brother, and never come back. There were rumours that Alec and Les Gill might have both been involved with the attack on the German troop convoy which had taken place that day out along the Middelbury Road. But they were not among the dead partisans dragged from the snow. And their names were not listed among the captives executed the following morning. But neither Alec Thrale nor Les Gill had ever returned. 'Oh, he's alive, Mildred,' Vera would say confidently. 'He'll have his reasons for not contacting us. Alec always has his reasons. And if Alec's alive then you may be sure that Les is too.' But Mill sometimes found it hard to share her friend's optimism. Her younger brother's disappearance still caused her pain. They had parted with misunderstanding and bitterness on Les's side and great anguish on hers. It was a hurt that had stayed with her. And, she was sure, would do so as long as she lived.

They ran across the lawn and up the steps of the Hall. The young men parted as they approached.

'He's hurt bad, Mrs Thrale,' said one.

'There's loads of blood,' said another.

Vera knelt down beside Phil Gingell. 'He's conscious,' she said. 'The first thing we must do is stop the bleeding.' She looked around and her eye fell on the flag which Phil had pulled from the wall. 'Perfect,' she said. 'Mildred?'

And Mill took out her penknife and began to tear the banner into bandages.

Chapter 9

There were still a dozen or so pale stars in the sky as Les stepped from the hut and pulled his coat around him.

'Wings' was already in the yard pumping up the tyres of the bicycles.

'Wonderful time of day, eh, Les?' he called.

Les shivered. 'Think so?'

'Oh, yes! You can watch the world start all over again. As though the slate's been wiped clean. The whole nasty business.' The airman pulled back his balaclava and looked up into the darkness. 'It looks so solid, doesn't it? Like a damned great lid. But it's not. It's a door. A door to another world. One that's clean. And empty. No one's messed about with it, you see? Best of all, no one owns it. At least, they shouldn't do. It belongs to whoever's up there for the time they're there and not a moment longer. You can roar about in it to your heart's content and so can anyone else but it's not yours and it's not theirs and . . . ' He stopped. And laughed. 'And from the look on your face it's the wrong day of the week for sermons.'

'Is that what it's like,' said Les, 'in a plane?'

'Even better. Listen, I'll take you up when this is all over. What d'you say?'

'All right.'

'Stout fellow.'

'I wish I was coming with you now.'

'Next time, eh? And you mustn't blame Gwen. She argued hard for you to come.'

'Why's Mervyn got it in for me?'

'Look, old sport, Mervyn's in charge, right? He's acting-

77

chief. It isn't personal. He's had a lot of experience in these things. If he had it in for you, believe me you wouldn't be standing here this morning.'

'Where is he?'

'The wizard? He took off earlier with his box of potions and charms. Eye of newt and stick of gelignite. Powerful magic. He and I don't always see eye to eye but he really is a wonder. Believe me, Harris and his pals won't know what's hit them. Ah, here's the lovely Gwen.'

'Everything ready?' she asked, as she came across the yard.

'Ready when you are, Queen of my Heart.'

'We're leaving everything in your care, Les,' she said.

'I'd still rather I was . . . '

'Les, guarding the camp is important.' She reached into the bag which was slung across her shoulder and took out a pistol. 'Here,' she said.

'For me?' he said.

'Take it.'

'Oh, thanks, Gwen! Thanks!'

'It's a Luger. I took it off a Jerry officer. Do you think you can manage it with that bandage on your hand?'

'Course! Thanks, Gwen.' And he wanted to throw his arms round her. Like a kid. So he didn't.

'We should be on our way,' said 'Wings', looking at his watch. 'We want to be in place before it's light.'

'Of course. Take care, Les,' she said. 'Oh, and keep an eye on the patient.'

He watched them wheel the bicycles up to the crest; and shortly afterwards they were lost from sight along the ridge.

Les slipped the Luger into his inside pocket. He let it sit there, enjoying its weight against his ribs. It was good to be trusted again. He stood for a while listening to the wind. Every now and then it caught a piece of loose corrugated metal on the roof of one of the huts and banged it noisily.

He turned to go back inside but hesitated in the doorway when he saw that the 'patient' was out of bed and leaning against the wall on the far side of the room.

'What d'you think you're doing?' he said.

The man turned unsteadily. 'Hello, son,' he said. 'Have they gone?'

'That's right.'

'I wanted to wish them luck,' he said. 'On your own, are you?'

'That's right.' Les took out the Luger, sat down at the table and began to check the ammunition clip.

The man watched him for a while. Then: 'I'm up and about,' he said.

'Yeah?'

'Yeah. You got family?'

'Not to speak of.'

'That's kept me going . . . on the road . . . in that camp . . . ' The man started towards the table but had only gone a step or two when he stumbled and sprawled headlong.

Les stood up. He waited. He wasn't sure what to do. But the man didn't move. Finally he walked across to him.

The man opened his eyes and looked up at him. He was breathing painfully and his deep-sunken eyes stared back helplessly. 'That's what I was doing,' he said. 'You know, when these people found me. Trying to get home . . . I can't get up.'

Les reached down and put an arm around the man's shoulder, lifting him to his feet. It was like picking up an empty suitcase. He carried him back to the bed and eased him down gently onto the straw.

'I was on my way,' said the man. 'I was going home.'

'You ain't ready to go home yet,' said Les.

'No. But soon, eh?' And the man's eyes closed.

What had they done to him? Les could still feel the shock the man's weight had given him. Starvation, that was. And Lord only knows what else!

Home, he'd said. Was that really what had kept him going? Through everything? And what about you, Les? What's kept you going, eh? Well, it ain't been 'home'. You ain't got no home, have you . . . not any more.

The insistent banging from the sheet of loose metal was

79

beginning to get on his nerves. He went over to the door. The dawn was approaching fast, bruising the clouds with yellow and grey. He could smell the morning. And . . .

What was that? Footsteps! Les fumbled for the Luger and gently slipped the safety-catch. Gently or not the sharp click seemed to echo round the yard. The footsteps stopped.

'Don't come any closer,' Les called. 'Stay where you are and identify yourself.'

There was no reply at first. And then a voice said: 'The light's behind you, boy; I could drop you any time I liked.'

'What?'

'You heard me. Throw down the gun.'

What a fool! The light from the open doorway made him a sitting target.

'Do it!'

Les placed the precious Luger on the ground.

'Kick it away from you,' came the order. 'And put your hands up.'

A dark figure came striding across the yard. He came quickly, stooped, and picked up the pistol. Then, as he straightened up, the light from the doorway fell on his bearded face.

Les stepped back in amazement.

'Stay still!' said the man.

'Mr Thrale?'

'What?'

'Mr Thrale? Mr Thrale, it's me!'

'What did you say?' The bearded man frowned. He reached out and turned Les's face towards the light. 'Leslie?' he said in astonishment. 'God Almighty, boy—is it? It is! It's you.'

'Mr Thrale! What are—'

'What are you doing here?'

'Guarding the camp.'

Alec Thrale shook his head. 'Well, I'm . . . young Leslie!' he said. 'Guarding the camp, d'you say? Then you'd better have this back.' And he handed Les the precious Luger.

They went inside and Alec sat down wearily at the table.

'Get that kettle on,' he said. 'And tell me how you come to be here.'

So Les made tea for them. And told his friend how it had all come about. About the leaflets. And the police station. And where Gwen and the rest were. And how he wished he was with them.

And Alec Thrale listened. The way Les remembered he always used to listen, looking to one side but hearing every word you said. And for a moment they might have been together again among Alec's traps and cages in the hut across the yard from Keeper's Cottage. And Vera would be in the kitchen. And Mill would come up the path from the village with her shopping-basket over her arm and . . .

'And Frank?' said Thrale. 'What about Frank? You was together up north, I believe.'

'Yes, we was. Then we got split up.'

'I've been on the move non-stop. Lose touch, did you?'

'For two years nearly . . . '

'Getaway?'

'But we met up again a few days ago.'

'What—you and Frank? You must have been pleased.'

Les nodded.

'Is he here with you?'

'No.'

'How come?'

'There was a Yank plane. It bombed the road we were on and . . . ' Les shrugged.

Alec frowned. 'I'm sorry to hear that, Leslie,' he said gravely. 'I truly am. You were good pals.'

'He saved my life. Remember? The day we attacked the convoy on the Middelbury Road?'

'I remember. Seems so long ago, don't it? That and Shevington and everything. And Mildred? Have you ever managed to contact your sister?'

Les shook his head.

'That's a pity. I've sent messages to Vera once or twice. Whether they ever got to her I don't know. And I couldn't exactly give her a forwarding address.'

Les filled Alec's mug. 'Have you been transferred to this unit?' he asked.

'This is my unit, Leslie.'

'Yours? What, you mean . . . ? Here, Mr Thrale, you ain't . . . you ain't never the chief, are you?'

Alec Thrale sipped his tea. 'I am.'

'And you've been away at that meeting they were talking about?'

'That's right.'

'Mr Thrale . . . '

But before Les could ask him any more there was a fit of coughing from the other side of the room and Thrale jumped to his feet, tugging his pistol from his belt.

'It's all right,' said Les quickly. 'It's all right. His name's Bill. They found him in the hills. He needed help, poor devil. He's escaped from one of them camps.'

Thrale gently lifted away the blanket and looked down at the man's face. 'God help us,' he said grimly; 'there's no faking that, is there?' He replaced the blanket and went back to the table. He sat down and rubbed his brow wearily, covering his eyes with his hands. 'He escaped from one of them places, did he?' he said. 'Then, by heaven, he'll need all the help anyone can give him.'

'You all right, Mr Thrale?'

'We come on one of them camps,' said Thrale quietly, 'a month and more ago . . . we were coming out of Wales up through the Black Mountains. It was tucked away in a valley you wouldn't have known was there. There must have been a couple of thousand men. The locals were doing their best to sort out anyone who was still alive. The guards had took to their heels. Though one or two of the slower ones had got themselves caught.'

'What did you do with them?'

'What they deserved.' Alec shook his head. 'I tell you, Leslie, I never thought I'd ever look on wickedness the like of that. Ah, but worse than that . . . I never thought I'd see men look so cold on the wickedness they'd done. Done with no real rage, as far as I could see; and no reason

82

neither. Well, not one I can make any sense of. Most of 'em done what they did to those poor blighters because they were told to, that was all. Worked them to death in blind obedience. Oh, there was a few fanatics and madmen and bullies but most of 'em . . . ' Alec Thrale shook his head again. 'I can't fathom it, Leslie; I can't fathom how a human being could behave like that. So . . . pitiless. Ah, and that others could devise such cruelty and order it done. It makes you . . . it makes you ashamed.'

Les waited but Alec did not go on.

They sat together silently as day began to spread across the sky. And outside, the metal sheeting went on banging in the wind.

While Alec Thrale slept, Les sat on the step of the hut waiting for the partisans to return. And while he sat, he remembered.

It wasn't something Les liked to do. He was usually able to find something to keep them at arm's length: memories. But now they came crowding in on him unsummoned and quite irresistible. And, to his surprise, he found he had no wish to resist them.

It must have been what that Bill had said about home, he thought; that must have been what started it. And then finding Mr Thrale—or, rather, Mr Thrale finding him.

Home.

What was that? The years he and his sister Mill had spent dodging the violent attentions of their mother and the fleeting visits of their merchant-sailor father in that buggy backroom beside the Thames hardly counted. Their lives then, like most of the people around them, had been mostly a matter of surviving.

And would he have survived without Mill? Without his older sister? Course not. When they were evacuated from London at the outbreak of war, she had been the one who'd insisted they were kept together. And when they were billeted with that evil couple in the sweetshop it was Mill who took the beatings. And when they'd run away and were on the road—those violent roads full of invading soldiers and desperate refugees—it was Mill who'd seen him through. And it was Mill who'd gone to the Thrales' door that day and asked for a drink of water.

It wasn't until Vera Thrale took them in, until they'd lived in the cottage with the gamekeeper and his wife, that they'd ever really had a home.

And when this was all over that's where Mr Thrale would go back to, wasn't it? To Keeper's Cottage. When the war was over. But not you, Les. No. You can't go back. Who's going to welcome you? Mill ain't going to be waiting with open arms, is she? And Vera? Vera would be bound to take Mill's side. Which was only fair. Cos Mill hadn't been the guilty party, had she?

No, Les, you was the guilty one! It was you. You forgot, didn't you? You forgot it all—everything. You forgot who Mill was and all the things she'd always been to you. You just forgot all about it. You just took one look and forgot everything . . .

He stood up suddenly. A walk. A walk would clear his head. Besides, time was getting on. Surely Gwen and the rest of them should be back by now? And for a terrible moment another possibility crossed his mind. What if they weren't coming back? What if it had all gone wrong? What if . . . ? He hurried across the yard. Walk. That was the answer. He'd walk up to the ridge and see if there was any sign of them.

He started up the slope and climbed quickly to the crest. He stood there shading his eyes and staring off in the direction of the town. His head was so full of Mill and the rest of it that it was a moment or two before he saw it. And at once he threw himself flat on the ground. It wasn't more than half a mile away. And it was really shifting. A police car. What should he do? Run back to camp? There wasn't time. He reached inside his jacket for the Luger. There was only one thing to do. He could hold them for a while. Mr Thrale would hear the shots and be able to get away.

He waited until the vehicle was only a few hundred yards from him and then he pulled out the Luger and jumped to his feet.

'Here! Over here!' he called.

The car skidded to a halt. They'd seen him. Someone started shouting. It'd be bullets next. Lead 'em away, Les! That was the trick. He turned to run.

'Come on, then!' he called.

'Les? Les?'

Les? The sound of his name made him hesitate. He looked quickly over his shoulder. Someone was waving from the running-board of the car. 'Les! Les!'

Les? It was Gwen. 'Gwen? Gwen!' he called. He waved back and ran towards the car. 'Wings' was at the wheel and Mervyn was sitting beside him carefully cradling a wooden box. Gwen jumped down. She had a rifle slung across her back.

'We did it,' she said. 'We did it, Les!'

'Wings' laughed and sounded the horn noisily. 'The wizard worked his magic! Didn't you, Merlin? Turned Harris and his minions into . . . what did you turn them into? Was it rats? Not much magic required in that case!' And he sounded the horn again.

But Mervyn didn't seem to share his high spirits. He got out and walked round to where Les was standing. 'What are you doing here?' he said.

Les grinned. 'Waiting for you.'

'God Almighty, can't you obey even the simplest order?'

'But . . . '

'You were told to look after the camp. "Wings", take the car and hide it in the hollow. Gwen, come with me. Quick now!' Mervyn started away down the slope. And Gwen and Les followed.

Alec Thrale was waiting by the door as they came into the yard.

'Success?'

'All accounted for, chief,' said Mervyn.

'And you've met our newest recruit?' said Gwen, nodding at Les.

'Les and I are old pals,' said Alec.

'You and Les?'

'Me and Les go back a while. So tell me how it went.'

They sat around the table and told him the details of the attack. How they'd driven the policemen deep into the building and given Mervyn the opportunity to lay his explosives. How they'd offered them all the chance to surrender. Most of them had. But not Commander Harris and his immediate staff. They had fought to the end; and been blown up when the time came. The rest? They'd been handed over to local volunteers.

'The Gifford's Mill people?' said Alec.

'Aye,' said Mervyn. 'There's a score and more of them now. They've been turning recruits away. Resistance has suddenly become very popular.'

'I'm pleased to hear it,' said Alec. 'Because we've other fish to fry.'

'Is there news, Alec?' said Gwen.

Alec nodded. 'Müller.'

Everyone looked at him. 'Müller? The Gauleiter?'

'The committee have ordered us to take him.'

''Struth!'

'Nothing would give me more pleasure, chief,' said Mervyn. 'But he's miles away.'

'Not any more. The rats are running for the side of the ship. Müller's heading this way. He's planning to get out secretly by air.'

'Who says so?'

'One of his own people. They're turning on each other faster than you can say Adolf Hitler.'

'It's a needle in a haystack, Alec.'

'I don't think so. There aren't many places locally where he can lie low. Not many places that would take him in.'

'There's only one where he'd be welcome.'

'There is. And that's where we'll watch for him.'

'And when he comes?'

'He mustn't be allowed to leave. Under any circumstances. That's the orders. Ah, "Wings"!'

'Alec! Good to see you.'

'What have you got there?'

'Wings' put down the suitcase he was carrying and threw open the lid. 'A few items I liberated from Harris's office,' he said, producing a ham, a bottle of brandy, and a truckle of cheese. The airman grinned. 'Permission to feast, chief?'

Alec smiled. 'Permission to feast. I reckon Müller will keep till the morning.'

Chapter 10

The voice from the wireless was overwhelmed by a hissing blizzard of static.

'Blast!' Simon Carey edged the tuner this way and that but couldn't find a clearer signal. 'Blast again!' he said. 'Of course, I don't listen to the music. It's all jitter-bugging and crooners. But I do try and listen out for the news bulletins. I mean, a lot of it's blatant propaganda but one can usually read between the lines.'

'Is it *Voice of America*?' said Frank. 'I used to listen to that.'

'Did you? Where?'

'Oh,' Frank shrugged, 'different places, you know.'

'I understand. I mean, I know it's illegal but you have to know what's going on, don't you? No, this is the American Army Network. Though I can pick up most stations in Europe. This is a jolly good wireless.' Simon laughed: 'German, naturally. Ah, listen . . . '

The static cut out abruptly and the voice of the announcer could be heard clearly again:

' . . . *where we are throwing back the enemy on all fronts! And now: News from the East.*

Support divisions of the Red Army advancing through Poland have captured and liberated a number of the Nazis' concentration camps. Reports describe the conditions under which the inmates were being held, mostly Jews deported from the occupied countries of Europe, as "truly a hell on earth". Despite the efforts of the guards to destroy or conceal their crimes, gas chambers and industrial ovens for the disposal of the victims of mass killings have been brought to light. Those who have survived . . . '

Simon reached over and turned it off.

'What did you do that for?' asked Frank

'Well, you can see what I mean about propaganda, can't you?'

'How do you mean?'

'Eric, the officers in the German army are gentlemen. That is not the way a gentleman would conduct a war. It's nothing more than very crude Russian propaganda.'

'Don't you believe it, then—the reports about what they've done?'

Simon laughed. 'Of course not,' he said. 'Do you?'

'There was a village near where I used to live,' said Frank, 'Middelbury it was called. There was a partisan lived there who took a bomb to the Jerries' headquarters in Shevington. He killed an SS officer. The general in charge, General von Schreier his name was, sent his men to the village and burned it down. All of it.'

'That sounds like a typical "atrocity" story to me, Eric.'

'But that's what von Schreier did. His soldiers took everyone away, Simon. I saw what was left. It was a ruin and everyone had been rounded up and transported.'

'I don't think so.'

'I saw the ruins. There was no one there.'

'No. I daresay if you were to look into it properly you'd find those people had just moved away. People are like that. Listen,' Simon opened a drawer and slipped some shotgun shells into his pocket, 'I'm going to take a scout round. But I think you'd better stay put. Why not come and look for me on the terrace in about an hour?'

And he went out.

The 'patient' was sitting up and Gwen was holding the plate for him. But he had the spoon and he was feeding himself.

'I feel so much better this morning,' he said.

'You're on the mend, Bill,' she said.

'Turned the corner, eh?'

'But you mustn't try to do too much. You have to take your time.'

'Oh, I can do that, all right,' he said. 'Cos I don't give up, you see? I got away from them twice. Did I tell you that? That's why they put me in that place. Cos I kept trying to escape. Keep trying, that's my motto. Consider Garibaldi!'

She laughed. 'What?'

'You know—Garibaldi,' he said. 'He never gave up.'

'Oh, I see.' She took the spoon from him and carried the empty plate across to the table.

'Do you have to go?' he said.

'Things to do,' she said.

'Shoot one for me,' he said.

'I will.'

Les was waiting with the bicycles. Gwen took hers and they walked up to the ridge together.

'How is he?' he said.

'He's doing well when you consider what he's been through. Those camps are . . . ' She shook her head. 'I don't think there is a word for them.'

'Were you with Alec when he found that one in Wales?'

She nodded. 'If our friend was in one like that he's lucky to be alive. But he's obviously a very stubborn man.'

'He wants to get home.'

'Is that what he told you?'

Les nodded.

'It's a nice thought,' she said. And they mounted the bikes and pedalled away along the crest of the hill.

Unlike Felicity, Simon never seemed to lock the door and Frank was able to come and go as he pleased.

He walked slowly to the end of the corridor and up a short flight of stairs where he found himself at the end of a high-ceilinged gallery with a balcony along one side. It was perfect.

Exercise was all he needed. He was making good

progress. The walking had really improved. He was more than halfway along the gallery in no time. Then something made him stop. There it was: that old feeling. The one he'd learned to trust implicitly. The life-saver. He was being watched. He was sure of it. But when he looked behind him the gallery was empty. And so was the balcony above.

Could he be imagining it? After all, it was the sort of place where you were bound to imagine things like that. More like a haunted castle than someone's house. The walls were lined with dark wooden panelling. There were suits of armour and carved oak chests at intervals on either side. And the ceiling was decorated like a church he'd once been in.

There it was again. Frank looked up. There was someone there! Up there, standing by the balcony rail.

'Felicity?' he called. 'Felicity, is that you?'

But Felicity Winfred Carey did not reply.

'What do you want?' he called.

'I thought you were my friend,' she said.

'What? I am . . . I . . . '

'No. You've forgotten all about me. I know you have.'

'Of course I haven't.'

'I hoped you weren't like everyone else, Eric. When I found you by that road I thought you must be special.'

'I am your friend. Honest.'

'I want to believe you, Eric. I want to believe you very much.'

'And I haven't forgotten you. Really.'

'Honestly?' She frowned. 'It's very important that you tell me the truth,' she said. 'Because I've something very, very important to tell to you. And I have to do so before Simon comes back. But . . . ' She hesitated. 'I'm sorry, Eric. I thought I would be able to tell you but I don't know if I can.'

'Felicity, if there's something I ought to know . . . '

'Go away, Eric,' she said suddenly.

'What?'

'You must. You mustn't wait a moment longer.'

91

'Why not?'

'Because they're going to come for us. And if you're here when they come . . . ' She hesitated.

'When who come?'

'Eric, they won't take you.'

'Who won't?'

She stamped her foot. 'You're not listening, are you? Please,' she said, 'please, please listen to me! Something horrible is going to happen to you, Eric, and I won't be able to stop it. I wish I could. I so wish I could. I want to so much. Promise me,' she said. 'Promise me that you'll go away.'

'Yes, all right.'

'This very minute?'

'Felicity, I can't—not this minute.'

'Soon then! Today!'

'Yes, all right, if that's what you want. But look . . . '

'Thank you.' She smiled. 'Goodbye,' she called and ran off along the balcony.

Simon was right, he thought, as he watched her, she was . . . she was unhinged, poor kid. But what was all that stuff she'd said about going away? That's what Simon had said, hadn't he? And he'd said it was a secret. Well, it was obviously some family thing. But what did she mean about something horrible happening?

When he reached the end of the gallery he found that the door there was locked. It didn't matter. The exercise was the important thing. He turned and began to walk back the way he had come. Every step was increasing his strength. At this rate it would be just a few more days and he would be ready.

'There's someone on the roof,' said Gwen.

'A lookout?'

'Possibly. Mind you, if Müller's coming, I don't think he'll come in daylight.' She lowered the binoculars and drew back into the evergreen shrubbery where they had taken up their position opposite the house. She handed the binoculars to Les. 'Keep your eyes skinned.'

Les slowly swept the house with the binoculars. The figure on the roof had withdrawn. Facing the gardens there was a terrace in front of some long windows but it was empty. And there was no movement at any of the windows elsewhere. Whoever was inside the house was lying very low indeed.

'You must have been really pleased to see Alec again, Les,' said Gwen. 'Being such old friends.'

'Him and Vera—that's Mrs Thrale—they was good to me. Taking me in, and that.'

'Do you miss Shevington?'

'I don't think about it.'

'And what about your sister?' said Gwen. 'Didn't you mention a sister the other day?'

'Did I?'

'Is she still there?'

He shrugged.

'Don't you know?' she said.

'Not for certain.'

She waited.

'Anyway,' he said, ' . . . it's not that.'

'What is it, then?'

'Nothing.'

'I see.'

'Something happened, that's all,' he said at last.

'Something bad?'

He nodded.

Again she waited.

'I saw 'em, you see?' he said. 'That's what started it. I saw 'em together.'

'Who?'

'Mill and this Jerry soldier. Mill's my sister.'

'A Jerry?'

'Yes. I saw 'em. Talking and walking about together. And I told her I had. And she told me she really liked him. Me and Mill, we had a bad falling out. Really bad.'

'Because she liked him?'

'Yes. No, not just cos of that.' Les turned away. 'We was hiding a wireless transmitter, you see,' he said, 'at Alec's cottage. It belonged to a chap called Crompton. He was an agent, one of ours. The Gestapo came looking for it. And this Jerry I'd seen her with . . . this young soldier . . . he was with 'em.'

'I see.'

'No, you don't. The thing is . . . when I saw he was with them . . . I just took it for granted it was Mill put them on to us.'

'That she'd betrayed you?'

He nodded.

'Had she?'

'No. Truth was, I heard afterwards she must have found out they was coming and she'd took the wireless and hid it somewhere else. So the Gestapo never found anything.'

'So what happened?'

'I ran off. To draw their fire.' Les turned suddenly and looked at her. 'But I'd let her see, Gwen,' he said. 'I'd let her see what I was thinking about her. She saw it in my face. Clear as day. Cos that's what I was thinking. I was thinking she'd done a thing as bad as that . . . me own sister . . . when all the time she'd done summat really brave.'

'But you didn't know that. I mean, I can see that might not have been the way it looked.'

'That's what Frank said. He said that.'

'He was right.'

'No!' said Les. 'That's no excuse! Not for thinking a thing like that . . . not about someone like Mill. And I know she still thinks that's what I think about her, I know she does. That's the worst thing.'

'I'm sure she doesn't.'

'No, p'raps she just thinks I'm dead and gone and good riddance!'

'Didn't you speak to her . . . after . . . '

'Things happened and I never went back. I couldn't.'

'When this is over . . . when you do go back to Shevington you can explain to her.'

'I ain't going back, Gwen.'

'When this is over it'll all look different. Isn't that why we're all doing this? I know I am. I'm going back, Les.'

'Are you . . . what, to Shropshire?'

'Yes. To my farm. Where I belong. You should go back, Les; to where you belong.'

'I don't belong nowhere . . . not no more.'

'But, Les . . . ' Gwen suddenly knelt up. 'Give me the glasses!' she said. 'Quickly! On the terrace! There, in front of the long windows! See? Two of them.' But Les didn't seem to have heard her. He was staring at the undergrowth not far from where they were hiding.

'Les?'

'No . . . ' he began.

'I didn't see them either,' she said. 'They must have come out while we were talking.'

'No! No,' he said, 'not them. There! Cover me, Gwen.' And he jumped up and ran from the thicket.

He didn't get far. The moment he emerged from the undergrowth there was a shout followed by two shots from a shotgun which turned Les and sent him scampering back.

Gwen grabbed his coat and hauled him away through the trees. She didn't stop until they'd reached the road.

'For God's sake, Les,' she said breathlessly, 'what were you playing at?'

'I had to,' he said.

'You exposed our position and nearly got yourself killed.'

'Gwen, I had to. Didn't you see it?'

'What? See what?'

'It was there. In the grass.'

'What was?' He was looking bewildered and shaking his head. 'Les, what was?'

'Frank's hat,' he said incredulously. 'Frank Tate's lucky hat.'

'What?'

'I'd know that hat anywhere. I know it don't make sense but . . . '

'It doesn't,' she said angrily. 'And you've told them we're here. Come on, we'd better get back to camp. We'll leave the Winscombe people to keep watch. Come on!'

Frank came running along the terrace. 'What were you firing at?' he asked.

Simon was quickly re-loading. 'Didn't you see him?' he said excitedly.

'See who?'

'They're getting so cocky. They attacked the police station in Charborough yesterday. We had a phone call warning us.'

'Who attacked the police station?'

'The partisans.' Simon pulled Frank inside and bolted the long windows. 'They're using the situation to stir up unrest—that's what father says.'

Frank laughed. 'They're not stirring up unrest, they're trying to liberate us.'

'Is that what you think?' Simon quickly drew the curtains across the windows. 'No, Eric—they're just doing what their masters tell them.'

Frank looked at him blankly. 'What do you mean?'

'Their masters. The people they're working for.'

'What people?'

'The Reds and the Jews! They're the ones behind all this.'

'But that's . . . '

'They're the ones behind all the trouble in the world. It's all so simple once you understand that. Mother and father explained it all to me ages ago. Mother's read all the books. So has Mrs Cato. Oh, yes! Mrs Cato's always been very sound. She's very clear about things. British Union of Fascists and all that. Right from the start. And, of course, father saw it all coming. He'd seen what strides they were making in Germany. He'd seen what had been accomplished. The Führer was building new factories faster than you could . . . well, jolly fast actually. And here father's factories were losing money hand over fist. Going to war against Germany was insane. Siding with ludicrous people like the Poles and the French. And those idiotic Americans. I mean, look what they did to you! And the Russians! How can Bolsheviks be our allies? They murdered the tsar. It's madness. It's a betrayal of all reason and decency. It's a betrayal of our blood, Eric. I'm going to find father. I'd keep clear of the windows, if I were you.'

Frank watched Simon hurry away. He was stunned. But that was Nazi talk, wasn't it? What Simon said was . . . Yes, you are . . . You're a bloody Nazi, Simon! Simon Carey was a bloody Nazi!

He turned and sprinted up the stairs. You mug, Frank Tate! You complete mug! That was what Felicity had been trying to tell him in her daft way, poor kid. She'd tried to warn him and he'd taken no notice. Her family were Nazi sympathizers. So what about Mr and Mrs Carey? And the housekeeper! They must be too. They all were! They were collaborators. Yes. And that stuff about going away . . . that was because they were going to do a bunk. There wasn't a moment to lose. It was time to get out. Time to make for Gifford's Mill and warn the partisans what was happening. The drop from the nanny's room was still the best bet. Into the stableyard. They wouldn't be expecting him to try that.

As he passed the window at the turn of the stairs he heard the sound of wheels on the gravel below. He looked down and saw a small car pull up in the drive. Three men got out and walked quickly towards the front door: a stooped, moustached figure in a shabby raincoat; a taller man in a dark suit; and a third man taking up the rear who wore a heavy overcoat. The overcoated man looked up at the house as they came up the steps. And Frank drew back quickly from the window.

He knew that face! That was . . . It was! That was the man he'd gone to the theatre to see. It was Connors: it was the actor who'd been 'Uncle' Herbert's courier.

Chapter 11

Frank ran to the landing above the entrance hall.

The other two had gone but the actor was still there. And Mrs Carey was with him.

'We weren't expecting another guest, Mr Connors,' Frank heard her say. 'I do apologize. If you'd just like to make yourself comfortable. I shan't be a moment.'

'So kind.'

Douglas Connors opened the door to the drawing room and gave a low whistle of approval. This place was the genuine article! It had real West End quality. It reminded him of the setting for the first act of *Sometimes in Ermine*. He'd understudied in that one. The summer of 1936. July. One of the leads. He'd actually 'gone on' the week Hilary Phelps had had his little bit of trouble. And damned good he'd been. Great things were expected to come of that week. Everyone had said so. Ah, well . . . What might have been!

He unbuttoned his overcoat and sank into one of the armchairs. Yes, indeed! This was a life to which he could very quickly become accustomed. But he wasn't going to get the chance, was he? He sighed. Here today and gone tomorrow. Quite literally. Ah well, life had always been a little like that. Had been, Douglas? Come, come— courage, dear boy! Nil desperandum!

He reached into his pocket for his cigarette case. There were only two scrawny roll-ups left. He got up and went over to the silver box on the mantelpiece. He opened it and sniffed the contents: Sullivan's Turkish! Wherever did they get Sullivan's Turkish in times like these? He began to fill his case from the box and then heard the door opening and closed the lid quickly.

'Hello,' he said brightly. And remembered that Schilte had mentioned something about a son. 'You must be young Carey.'

'No,' said the boy, 'Simon's . . . Look, it doesn't matter; there's not much time. I've got to talk to you.'

'By all means.' Why was the boy staring like that?

'Don't you remember me?'

'Should I?' said the actor.

'You gave me your autograph.'

'My dear chap, you and so many others.'

'But don't you remember? It wasn't for me. It was for my uncle . . . Herbert Sillitoe.'

Connors felt his mouth go dry. Good God! Now he recognized him. It was the boy who'd come to the stage door that night! 'Yes. Yes, of course,' he said, recovering himself. 'Of course I remember you. Do forgive me. What in heaven's name are you doing here?'

'Have you been sent to capture the Nazis?'

'The Nazis?'

'The Careys. They're going to do a bunk. Have you come to stop them?'

'Stop them?' Of course, the boy thought he was still working for Sillitoe's lot! 'Yes! Yes, of course. That's the plan. Tell me, are you armed?'

'No. I've only just found out about them. I was going to make a run for it but . . . '

'No, you mustn't do that.'

The door opened and Rowena Carey and Mrs Cato came in.

'Mr Connors . . . ' Rowena began and then saw Frank. 'Eric?' she said sharply. 'What are you doing here?'

Connors looked from one to the other. What a good question, Mrs Carey, he thought. But one that I think we'll leave unanswered until the waters are a little less muddy. 'My fault, Mrs Carey,' he said; 'I do apologize. I stepped out into the hall and saw the boy passing and we got chatting—you know, the way one does.'

'I really must ask you to keep to your room, Eric,' she said. 'There are family matters we have to attend to. Please go back upstairs.'

She watched Frank leave and glanced across at Mrs Cato. Then she turned to Connors. 'I hope you didn't mention anything important to him?' she said.

'Just chewing the fat.'

'That boy has no part in our plans.'

'I was the acme of discretion.'

'I'm pleased to hear it. Your room is ready now. Dinner is at eight.'

'Most kind.' And Douglas Connors smiled his most disarming smile.

'If you'd like to follow me, sir,' said Mrs Cato icily.

Alec Thrale was sitting on the hill above the camp searching the sky with his binoculars. He turned as Les climbed up towards him.

'You wanted to see me, Mr Thrale?'

'Gwen's told me what happened. What have you got to say for yourself?'

'Sorry, Mr Thrale.'

'Is that it?'

'She doesn't understand,' said Les, sitting down next to him. 'She can't, can she? Frank was my mate. He was my best mate. You know that, Mr Thrale. You know what good pals we were.'

'What's that got to do with it?'

The question took Les by surprise. 'But . . . don't you see? I thought it was Frank's hat,' he said. 'I was sure it was . . . and I thought Frank was dead. I don't think he is any more. I thought you'd understand, Mr Thrale.'

'You don't think, Leslie. That's your trouble.'

'Be fair. I thought he must still be alive . . . don't that matter?'

'No, Leslie,' said Thrale flatly, 'it don't.'

'But, Mr Thrale . . . '

100

'There's only one thing that matters. And that's the thing men and women have been fighting for for the last four years. And until that's accomplished nothing else matters. I thought you understood that.'

'Frank was . . . '

'Frank's gone, Leslie. That's over and done with. And we've been given a job to do. Oh, there's bigger murderers than Müller—plenty—but he's our responsibility. And it's a responsibility I take very seriously; and so does everyone in this unit. Do you?'

'Course!' said Les.

'No, Leslie! There's no "course" about it. What you did endangered that job and the life of your comrade. And you did it on a whim. A fancy!'

'I'm sorry, Mr Thrale.'

'You've let me down. I want you to assure me that from now on you'll obey orders to the letter.'

'I do obey orders,' said Les, and got to his feet indignantly.

'Did the Gifford's Mill people send you to the top of that church tower? Well?'

Les shook his head.

'I didn't think they did. I need discipline from you, Leslie. That's if you're to remain as part of this unit. D'you understand? I want your word.'

'Yes, Mr Thrale.'

'Good. Then we'll say no more.'

Les started back down the hill. He turned after a few steps. 'You comin' in?' he asked.

But Alec Thrale did not reply. He lifted the binoculars and went back to slowly quartering the skies.

Simon Carey grimaced at the mirror as he tugged the ends of his bow tie this way and that.

'Blast,' he said. 'Double-blast!' He pulled the tie apart and began to knot it for the umpteenth time. 'It's got to be absolutely right this evening.'

'What's so special about this evening?' Frank asked.

'Eric, I'd love to tell you, honestly. Because it's going to be very, very special. It really is. But I'm afraid I can't.'

Finally he seemed satisfied with his efforts. 'There! What do you think?'

'Looks all right to me,' said Frank.

Simon took a last look in the mirror. 'Listen,' he said, 'you didn't mind me being so straightforward with you earlier, did you? You know, about where we Careys stand? The rights and wrongs of the situation?'

'No. Course not.'

'Splendid. I didn't think you'd be the sort to get all hot and bothered about it. Matter of fact, Eric, you seem quite a decent fellow. Which is why I feel a bit awkward about . . . Look, the fact is, this is a family matter, d'you see? What I mean is, it's rather private: the meal tonight, I mean.'

'Fair enough.'

'You don't mind having to stay here? In the room?'

'No.'

'Oh.' Simon seemed almost disappointed. 'Yes, but . . . Oh, look here,' he said, 'I don't suppose it'd hurt if you came to the top of the stairs for a quick look. Would you like that?'

'If you like.'

'But whatever you do don't let anyone see you.'

They walked together to the top of the stairs. And Frank watched Simon hurry down and disappear into the drawing room. Not long after, the doors opened and Mrs Carey came out. She was wearing an elegant evening gown and there were jewels on her wrist and neck. She had taken the arm of a man in a dark uniform and highly-polished jackboots. The odd thing was, Frank was sure the man hadn't been one of the two who had arrived with Connors. He didn't look like either of them. The other man was there: he was the one next to Mr Carey. And then came Simon and Connors. Felicity had fallen behind. Mrs Cato was waiting at the door of the dining room. As the uniformed man approached she raised her hand in salute.

'Heil Hitler!'

'Heil Hitler!' he replied.

Then the doors closed behind them.

The dining room curtains had been drawn across the long windows, shutting out the night. Hurricane lamps burned on the mantelpiece and there were others arranged around the walls. The dinner table, covered in a dazzling damask cloth, was laid with elegant silver cutlery and the Careys' finest Sèvres service. Two elaborate silver candelabra blazed in the centre of the table creating a cavern of golden light which enclosed the Careys and their guests.

If one squinted, Connors mused, and if one ignored the smell of the hurricane lamps, it was a picture of elegance and refinement. The wine was first class. And the food— served discreetly by the grim old duck in the starched apron—was plain but tasty; and there was plenty of it.

Connors had been placed between the children. Which was obviously where the lady of the house thought he belonged. The girl hadn't said a word since the meal began; and despite all his attempts at banter the boy seemed far more interested in what they could hear of the conversation at the other end of the table.

'I must say it's a relief to see you looking yourself again, Gauleiter,' Hugh Carey observed. 'I hardly recognized you when you arrived this afternoon.'

Of the stooped, moustached figure in the shabby raincoat who had hurried up the steps some hours before nothing remained. At the head of the table sat a thick-set figure in the black uniform of the SS. His corn-coloured hair was combed back in an abrupt line from his forehead. The pale face beneath was clean-shaven, his eyes still and blue, and his mouth a small, narrow line which when it smiled hardly lengthened at all.

'We must thank Mr Connors for so successful a deception,' the Gauleiter replied.

'Too kind,' said Connors. 'It's the make-up I used as the

insurance salesman in *Norwich Union*. He wasn't all he appeared to be either.' The actor laughed but the joke seemed lost on the Gauleiter. 'He turned out to be the heroine's long-lost brother,' Connors explained. 'In the final act he saves her from an unfortunate marriage.'

Rowena Carey turned to Schilte. 'I imagine we'll be restricted as to what we can take with us, Herr Schilte?' she said.

'Alas, Mrs Carey, it is inevitable. A small suitcase will be all our journey allows. An invidious choice, I think, to pack one's life into such a small space?'

'Not at all.' She smiled. 'Our lives are beginning again, Herr Schilte.'

'And it's still going to be tomorrow, is it?' said Hugh. 'No change there?'

Schilte nodded. 'Oh, yes—everything remains exactly as arranged.'

Connors helped himself to another glass of the excellent burgundy—if he waited for the old duck to refill his glass he was quite convinced he'd die of thirst—and tried again to talk to Simon.

'An old chum, is he?' he said casually. 'The other young chap . . . whatsisname?'

'You mean Eric?'

'Yes, that's right. Friend from school?'

'Good heavens, no!' Simon sounded rather indignant. 'He's not a friend of mine. My sister found him.'

'Found him?' Connors laughed and turned to Felicity. 'Did you really? Where?'

'On a battlefield,' she said without looking at him.

'Good heavens! I say, what larks! A battlefield?' But Felicity continued to avoid his glance and said nothing. Good Lord, the child was serious! 'I see,' said Connors. 'And what was he doing on this battlefield?'

This time Felicity seemed about to reply but before she could do so her mother called from the other end of the table: 'Simon, dear?'

'Yes, mother?'

'Simon, dear, I've been telling the Gauleiter about your deep admiration for the *Germania* of Tacitus.'

'Me, mother?' And Connors could have sworn the boy blushed.

'I am not an educated man, of course,' said Müller. 'No, no . . . ' he waved away Mrs Carey's attempt to contradict him. 'But the *Germania* has always been a source of inspiration both to me and to the Movement. As a youth, I and many like me drew great strength from it. It speaks so eloquently of the German people and their civilization. It is all there. All that the Roman saw in us so long ago. The things that made us unique and powerful then. That still do. The things that have made us what we are. You see, young man, it was obvious to Tacitus even then what it was that made the German race so superior. As I remember . . . You will correct me if I am wrong, Mrs Carey?'

Rowena Carey smiled.

Oh, come now, thought Connors; you're not the sort of man anyone corrects.

The Gauleiter closed his eyes: 'Yes, as I remember,' he said slowly, 'the Roman tells us "the peoples of Germany have never been tainted by intermarriage with other races, and stand out as a nation peculiar, unspoilt and unique of its kind . . . "'

'Their blood is pure!' Simon interrupted enthusiastically. 'That's the thing, isn't it?'

'Simon!' hissed his mother. But Simon wouldn't be stopped.

'And that's the important thing. Some people's blood is cleaner than other people's. And that's what makes them better than other people . . . ' Simon Carey faltered. 'Doesn't it?'

The Gauleiter fixed the boy with his gaze. And the table waited. 'You speak well, young man,' he said solemnly. 'And if you are forced to forget all else always remember that. Always.' He smiled. 'You are intrigued by my Oak Tree?' he said, indicating the decoration he wore at his throat: a small, diamond-studded oak tree on a ribbon of red, white, and black.

'I am, sir,' said Simon. 'I know most of the uniforms. In some detail. And all the medals. But your oak tree . . . '

'It is the insignia of the Companions of Arminius. A select band of warriors bound by blood oath to defend the Fatherland to death . . . and beyond. Do you know who Arminius was? Under his leadership the Cherusci wiped out an entire Roman army. Wiped them out. Not a man of them survived. They were lured deeper and deeper into our dark German forests and eradicated. The piles of their bones rose as high as the housetops.'

'Gosh!'

'You will find that in Tacitus too. The *Annals* not the *Germania*.'

'It's not a decoration I've ever seen before, Gauleiter,' said Hugh.

'I wear it only on the most special occasions. I thought it appropriate to wear it tonight.'

'You honour us, Gauleiter,' said Rowena.

'We Germans are people of the forests, Mrs Carey. In the timeless forests lies the source of our strength.'

'And Adolf Hitler is our Arminius!'

They all turned to where Mrs Cato stood with her hands clasped in front of her. 'The Leader will give us victory,' she said. 'Let our enemies come just like the Romans.'

The Gauleiter seemed moved by the housekeeper's interruption. For a moment or two he toyed with his napkin-ring, tapping his finger on the table beside it, as though he was trying to make his mind up about something. Finally: 'You see further than you know, Frau Cato,' he said. 'And let me tell you why. Even as I speak the Führer is preparing to launch a weapon that will eradicate our enemies for once and for ever. A weapon of supreme vengeance and power that will place the German people and their allies finally at the summit of the world. In a matter of weeks, I can assure you beyond all possible doubt, our triumph will be final and complete. Forgive me, I have said far too much.'

'Not at all, Gauleiter,' said Hugh Carey enthusiastically.

Connors glanced up the table to where Müller was sitting. Did the nasty little man really believe all that? Did he? Yes, he did. You could see it in his eyes. It—or something. Some faraway light. Shining through the tall pine trees. Steady, Douglas—at least you've done what you've done for the price of a decent meal; and not because you believed any of this tosh. Timeless forests, dead Roman legions, and racial purity! They were mad as hatters—and a damned sight more dangerous—the whole pack of them!

'I offer you this promise,' said Müller, 'you who sit with me around this table. I do so because I know that I am among friends. Friends who share our values and goals. You, Herr Carey, whose contribution to our industrial effort has been so crucial. And you, dear Frau Carey, who has never failed to make us welcome here in your beautiful home and to restore us with your hospitality and keen mind. You are friends who have walked with us this far and you will be beside us at the dawning of the longed-for day.'

'We have followed in absolute confidence, Gauleiter,' said Mrs Carey. 'We have been faithful.'

The Gauleiter took her hand. 'Stay faithful. Only a little further. Tomorrow the world will be ours.' He pushed back his chair and got to his feet. 'Final victory,' he said and lifted his glass.

'Final victory!' they chorused.

'Final victory!' echoed Connors enthusiastically. And wondered if that boy . . . what was his name? Eric? He wondered if Eric had been wise enough to prepare an escape route.

Chapter 12

The Benny Goodman Band bounced through the final bars of 'Sing, Sing, Sing!' And as the last notes died away the voice of the announcer broke in:

'Good evening, Europe! This is the American Forces Network. And this is Chuck Eschle bringing you the latest bulletin hot from our armies fighting on all fronts.

As of fifteen hundred hours this afternoon our armoured divisions have secured bridgeheads all along the Rhine. We have begun crossing into Hitler's Fatherland! The troops of the First and Ninth Armies are advancing into the Rühr. The enemy are falling back on a front stretching from Krefeld to Koblenz.

Keep on runnin', Fritz! Cos mighty soon there's gonna be no place to run to.

And here's a message for all you folks over there in Britain. Keep your pecker up, old boy! The Yanks are coming!

Wish there was more time to jaw but we've a war to win. Back on the hour same spot on the dial!

And now, for your listening pleasure, the honeycomb tones of the lovely Jo Stafford . . . '

'The Yanks are certainly moving fast,' said Gwen.

'Giving Adolf a taste of his own blitzkrieg,' said 'Wings'.

She watched him and smiled as, for the third time, he aimed the thick woollen yarn at the eye of the darning needle.

'Never mind the Rühr. Holland's the door they have to close,' said Mervyn. He was sitting at the table, his spectacles perched on the end of his nose, preparing fuses by the glow of an oil-lamp. 'You're in my light, boy.'

Les shifted along the bench. He was happy to retreat

into the shadows. They all knew what he'd done. No one had said anything but they all knew. He'd behaved like a kid. That's what they must all think of him. Alec, Mervyn, 'Wings' . . . Gwen! Still, they hadn't seen that hat, had they? Or, maybe . . . Oh, what was the use? Maybe it was just because he'd been talking about Shevington to Gwen. Maybe that's what had made him think about Frank and thinking about Frank had made him think . . .

'Hold that for me.'

He looked up to find Mervyn was offering him a short length of wire.

'Take it, boy. I haven't got three pairs of hands.'

Les took the wire and watched Mervyn carefully crimp it at one end.

'Feeling sorry for yourself, are you?' said the Welshman.

'No,' said Les quickly.

'Discipline, Les Gill. Hate as much as you like, nobody's stopping you. But above all—discipline. If you've learned that lesson you'll be welcome here. And we might all even survive. Aye, we might even win this war.'

'We are going to win it,' said Les.

'And what makes you think that?'

'Cos . . . cos we're right.'

'You think so, do you? I'm glad to hear it. But being right doesn't mean you win. We learned that the hard way in Spain.'

Mervyn took the wire and laid it carefully alongside the others in his wooden box.

'Are they to blow up Müller?' Les asked.

'No, they're not,' came the reply. 'I want him alive. I want him to answer for his crimes at the bar of history. That's what they've got to do, the whole murdering Nazi crew. Aye, and all their pals. But failing that, it must be said . . . ' And Les could have sworn that Mervyn smiled—'it'd give me great satisfaction to blow the bloody lot of them sky high.'

'Wings' looked up from his darning. 'When do you think the Yanks'll land, Mervyn?' he said. 'Prophesy for us, O Wise One!'

'They can come whenever they like,' said Mervyn. 'As long as it's not before we've taken Müller. He's ours. Meanwhile they should shut the door to Holland and stop the Germans reinforcing.'

'Wings' sighed and put down the needle and yarn. 'I give up,' he said. And caught Gwen's eye. 'Gwen, you don't think . . . '

'No, I don't,' she said. And laughed. 'Consider Garibaldi!'

'Garibaldi?' he said. 'Whatever for?'

'Because he never gave up.'

'Wings' grinned. 'Oh, I see what you mean.'

'Gwen?' Les was on his feet.

'What?'

'Gwen,' he said, 'why did you say that?'

'Because it's time "Wings" learned to thread a needle and darn his own socks, that's why.'

'No. Why did you say "Consider Garibaldi" like that?'

'I don't know. Someone said it to me recently and it seems to have stuck in my head. It's rather a good motto, don't you think?'

'Who? Gwen, who said it to you?'

'I can't remember. I think it was . . . ' She turned and indicated the straw where 'the patient' was asleep. 'Yes, it was our friend Bill over there. Les? Les, don't—he's asleep.'

But Les was already at the man's side and shaking him awake.

The man opened his eyes and struggled to sit upright in the straw. 'What? What do you want?' he said anxiously. 'What is it?'

'Why did you say that?' demanded Les. 'What you said to Gwen?'

'What?'

'Consider Garibaldi! What did you say that for?'

'Because . . . because Garibaldi never gave up . . . '

'I know he never,' said Les. 'But why did you say it?'

Gwen was next to him now and trying to restrain him.

And the others were staring at him. 'Les,' she said, 'take it easy.'

'Just tell me why you said it. Please?'

'It's what my mother used to say,' said the man in the straw.

'Your mother?'

'Yes.'

'What's your name?'

'Tate,' the man replied; 'my name's Bill Tate. Why? What's the matter?'

Les stood up. He backed slowly away and then turned and ran out of the hut.

It must have been the Gifford's Mill people who'd sent Connors. It must have been one of their men Simon had shot at. And Connors must have a plan. He was down there now in the middle of the Nasties eating and drinking. He must have a plan. He wouldn't have walked into this nest of vipers without one.

Frank turned off the wireless and began pacing backwards and forwards in front of the window.

Now that he knew about Simon and the rest of them it all made sense, of course. All that stuff about not leaving the house. It was the partisans the Careys were afraid of. And about someone coming to take them away. Someone was coming to help them do a bunk.

But what about Felicity? Felicity and her wishbone? And her knights in armour? And her foxtrot? Wasn't that what she'd said? That she'd almost mastered the foxtrot?

And he'd told her how his cousin Rose was a good dancer too. Oh, Rose could dance! He could see her now dancing in Nan Tate's tiny kitchen and making them all laugh. Even Edie, her mother, who never laughed much, laughed at Rose. Lovely, lively Rose. He'd liked Rose most of all. Well, next to Nan. Would Rose, or any of the Worths, still be in Shevington when this was all over?

Would Shevington even be there when this was all over?

Or might it have suffered the same fate as Middelbury? Razed to the ground. Wiped off the map as if it had never existed. That was what the Nazis had done to Middelbury, and all because someone had lifted their fist against them. Because of that the heel had come down on Middelbury and everyone who lived there. He would never forget the day he had come cycling over the hill and seen it there below him. Like a snow-covered cemetery. Deserted. No— it wasn't deserted. He'd felt them there. Standing in what had once been the village High Street. So many ghostly presences. Staring at him. Pleading mutely to be remembered. Not to be forgotten.

Come on, Mr Connors—where are you?

'Mr Thrale, it's got to be him!'

'Like that hat had to be Frank's hat?'

'This is different,' insisted Les. 'How else would he know about Garibaldi? That was Nan Tate's saying.'

'He don't look like the Bill Tate I recall.'

'Well, he wouldn't, would he? Not after . . . not after so long and what he's been through. Come and talk to him, Mr Thrale, please?'

As Alec and Les came into the hut, Alec handed 'Wings' the binoculars. 'Take over the watch for a spell, will you?' he said.

'Right ho, chief.'

Alec walked over to the table where Bill Tate was sitting. 'How're you doing, friend?' he said.

Bill Tate looked up. He had a blanket round his shoulders and was sipping the mug of tea Gwen had given him.

'I'll survive,' he said.

'We've not had much time to get acquainted.'

'That's all right. You're Alec, I know that,' said the patient. 'You're the chief.'

'And your name's Tate, is it?'

'That's right. Bill, Bill Tate.'

'And this "Consider Garibaldi" business,' said Alec.

Bill Tate frowned. 'What about it?'

'Les tells me you told him it was something your mother used to say.'

'Yes. We had a picture of Garibaldi on the wall. In the kitchen.'

'And where was that?'

'That was Shevington. West Sussex way.'

'So you're from Shevington?' said Alec.

'Yes. Shevington born and bred. Though I left the old place a few years ago now. When I got married. Look, what's all the fuss about?'

'No particular fuss,' said Alec. 'Just interested. You don't remember me, do you?'

'Should I?'

'It's possible. My name's Thrale.'

'Thrale? Not Alec Thrale? No! You're never Sam Thrale's boy? The gamekeeper at the Hall?'

Alec nodded.

'Alec Thrale! Well I'm blessed! No, I didn't know you. Not with the beard. Well I'm damned.'

'I can't say I recognized you either.'

'Well, I'm not looking my best, am I?' Bill Tate replied.

'So what happened to you?'

'I was captured. September 1940. In Seabourne. I was living there with my boy Frank. I was firewatching the night they landed. At the factory where I worked. We didn't have a chance. The Jerries wanted me to go on working there but I refused and they shipped me off to one of their road gangs. I was on that for a couple of years. Then I escaped. But they caught me. And I escaped again. That's when they sent me to that camp. Lancashire way. That's where I've been. S'posed to be building a dam.'

'Did you escape?'

'Nobody escaped from that place. It wasn't just people like me, you see; there were all sorts. We had French and Poles—politicals. And soldiers who'd been took prisoner in Russia. They had the worst of it; they treated them like animals. No, you wouldn't treat an animal the way they treated them. They said they weren't proper human beings, you see? So they worked them till they died. Them and plenty of others. That's what all their flags and fancy uniforms and shouting comes down to in the end . . . treating people like they're less than animals. Anyway, we woke up one morning—it must be almost a month ago now—and the Jerries had gone. They'd just piled into lorries and run for it. Me and two other chaps started walking south. But the other two were in bad shape. They gave up.'

'But not you?'

'No. I don't give up easy.'

'Alec?'

'Wings' had come back into the hut. And he wasn't alone.

'This chap's from Winscombe,' he said.

Alec stood up. 'News?'

'There was a car turned up at the house late this after-noon,' said the newcomer.

Mervyn slapped the table. 'It's him!'

'There were three passengers. But we didn't get a very good look at them.'

'But one of them was Müller?'

The newcomer shook his head. 'None of them looked like Müller. I mean, I've only seen photos of him in the papers but none of 'em looked like him. Not really.'

'Alec?' said Gwen.

'Dammit, it must be him!'

'What do we do?'

'I say we attack anyhow,' said Mervyn. 'Alec?'

'I don't know. We could lose him completely if it's not him and we close off his bolt-hole.'

'I'd know him.'

They all turned to look at Bill Tate.

'What do you mean?' said Alec.

'Gauleiter Müller? Is it him you're after?'

'That's right.'

'I'd know him.'

'How come?'

114

'He used to visit the camp. "Inspections" they called it. To make sure we were being worked hard enough. Oh, yes, I'd know Gauleiter Müller.'

'Would you come with us?' said Alec. 'To Winscombe?'

'Alec,' said Gwen, 'he's in no state to . . . '

'Never mind that. Do you reckon you're up to it, Bill Tate?'

'I'd crawl there on my knees to see that swine get his come-uppance.'

'Good man. Are your people still watching the house?' said Alec turning to the Winscombe man.

'Careys can't cut a slice of bread without us knowing it.'

'Keep it that way. Mervyn?'

Mervyn tapped his box of tricks. 'Ever ready.'

'They won't try to fly him out at night. Not with the landing problems they're going to have. We'll go for him tomorrow morning.'

'In that case, Bill, you'd better get some rest,' said Gwen. 'Les?'

Les offered Bill Tate his arm and helped him up.

'How come you knew my mother then, Les?' said Bill. 'You don't sound like a Shevington man.'

Les looked uncomfortable.

'Les lived in Shevington for a while,' said Alec. 'With my wife and me.'

'Well, I never!'

'He was an evacuee.'

'Getaway! And you heard Nan Tate say "Consider Garibaldi"?'

'Yes,' said Les. 'Yes, lots of times.'

Bill Tate stopped. 'Listen, my boy Frank wasn't there, was he? It's where I always told him to go to if ever we got split up. I don't suppose . . . '

'If you're coming with us in the morning you must get some rest,' said Gwen quickly. 'You can talk to Les later.'

'Yes,' he said. 'Yes, I'll do that. Thanks, Les.'

Bill Tate lay down on the straw and they covered him with the blanket.

'You're going have to tell him, Les,' said Gwen as they walked back to the table.

'Gwen, I can't.'

'You've got to.'

'I can't, Gwen. How can I tell him Frank's dead?'

Chapter 13

Connors was standing outside the door. And seemed to be listening. He turned guiltily when Frank called.

'Eric!' he said. 'There you are. The very man I was looking for. I wasn't sure which room you were in.'

'I'm along there. In with Simon,' Frank replied. 'Is everything all right?'

'Couldn't be better. But I wanted to explain to you about last night.' He took Frank's arm and walked him away from the door. 'It must have looked a bit odd, my hobnobbing with those blighters. But you know how it is in this business. One has to play them along.'

'I knew you must have a plan.'

'Exactly. Tell me, are you allowed to leave the house? We may need to get information out, you see.'

'I think Simon's supposed to keep an eye on me. But I know a way.'

'Good man!'

'It's out through the window of the nanny's room.'

'And where's that?'

'It's the other side of Felicity's room. Listen, it was on the wireless last night, the Yanks have crossed into Germany. They're advancing on all fronts.'

'Splendid.'

'The Careys and those Nazis will have to go soon.'

'Yes, they will, won't they. Now, listen . . . ' Connors turned, as the door where he had been standing opened and Hugh Carey came out. 'Dreary sort of morning, Mr Carey,' he said.

'What's that?' said Hugh abstractedly. 'Oh, yes. The rain.' And he hurried on.

Connors frowned. 'Did you see him, Eric? That is a worried man. Very worried. I wonder what's afoot? I'm going to take a scout round.'

'Shall I come with you?'

'No. No, you stay in your room. I may need to find you quickly. And, remember, play them along. They mustn't have any suspicion what we're doing here.'

Reinhardt Schilte was lingering over breakfast.

'Is there any more of your delicious preserve, Mrs Cato?' he enquired.

'Of course, Herr Schilte,' the housekeeper replied. 'I'll bring some at once.'

'Mrs Cato?'

'Herr Schilte?'

'We were all greatly impressed last night,' he said. 'By the sentiments you expressed. The Reich has a special place for loyalty of that kind.'

'Thank you, sir,' she said. 'I ask no more than that.'

As she went out Hugh Carey came in. 'Schilte?' he said.

'Mr Carey?'

'Schilte, the telephone is dead. I can't raise the Exchange.'

'Are you certain?'

'It's stone dead. Do you think the terrorists have cut the wire?'

'It's what I would do.'

'Surely this means they're going to try something soon.'

'I doubt they will attack in daylight. Excuse me, but I must speak to the Gauleiter.'

'Herr Schilte? May I . . . '

'Be quick, please.'

'I rather wondered what time we were going to leave.'

'All in good time, Mr Carey. Meanwhile please prepare yourselves for an instant departure. Now, if you'll excuse me.'

Hugh Carey went over to the window and looked out at the rain. They were out there. They were out there

118

waiting. To take their revenge. And time was getting short.

'Has Herr Schilte gone, Mr Hugh?' Mrs Cato had brought a pot of her quince jam.

'Yes, Mrs Cato,' he replied, 'yes, he has. Things seem to be starting to move.'

Rowena Carey looked up as the door opened.

'What is it, Felicity?' she asked. 'And why are you dressed like that?'

Felicity Carey was wearing her navy raincoat, a long scarf, and her beret was pulled down over her ears.

'You told me to be ready to leave,' she said.

'But where's your case?'

'I don't need one. This all I'm taking.' Felicity indicated the book she was carrying.

'Felicity, please don't be obtuse. Not at a time like this.'

'I'm not, mother. And the rest is in here.' She tapped the pocket of her raincoat.

'Felicity, you're being very silly. Go and pack properly. And you don't need to bring that wretched book with you. There'll be plenty of good books where we're going. Off you go.'

Mrs Carey knelt down and began to fasten the suitcase; but the door opened again almost as soon as Felicity had gone out and her husband came in.

'Hugh!' she said irritably. 'Hugh, I'm trying to finish the packing.'

'They've cut the telephone wires,' he said.

She stood up quickly. 'What does Schilte say?'

'He doesn't seem unduly perturbed. He says they won't attack in daylight.'

'We must hope not. And what about the boy?'

Hugh Carey turned away. 'I don't know, Rowena,' he said. 'I don't know what to do about the boy.'

'Hugh?'

He paused, leaning against the door. 'But, my dear, he's not a danger.'

'He's an unnecessary complication,' she said. 'It's bad enough having to take this Connors person with us. Hugh, we are being evacuated because of our proven loyalty. No one else was included in the arrangement. I'm not asking you to do anything yourself. Please speak to Schilte. He is clearly the sort of man who's used to dealing with situations like this.'

'Very well.'

'And meanwhile, Hugh.'

'Yes, my dear?'

'I think you should lock Eric in his room.'

With a flick of the clothes-brush Gauleiter Heinrich Müller removed an irritating suspicion of last-night's cigar ash from the lapel of his uniform. Then he replaced it on its hanger and hooked it over the picture rail.

He turned and considered himself in the mirror on the wardrobe door. The shabby, three-piece suit and nondescript shirt and tie had been well-chosen. He looked like a pen-pusher, he decided. Some pathetic clerk in a dusty office. A nonentity. A man of no importance whatsoever.

'How much longer, Schilte?' he asked, glancing at his watch.

Schilte looked up from the map he had spread on the counterpane. 'An hour, Gauleiter. Less. We must hope this cloud disperses.'

'Rain will not deter our intrepid flyers, Schilte. Have you dealt with the telephone?'

'Carey is convinced it was the terrorists.'

'Good.'

There was a knock at the door.

'Come!' the Gauleiter called.

'Are you ready, Gauleiter Müller?'

'You are most punctual, Mr Connors. Yes, come in.'

Müller made himself comfortable in the chair opposite the mirror. And Connors opened the make-up box.

'As before?' he enquired.

120

'Oh, yes—exactly as before.'

'I did wonder whether you'd need the full fig. For a journey like this one.'

'We never leave anything to chance, Mr Connors.' Müller closed his eyes while Connors deftly rubbed the colour into his cheeks. 'Nothing has ever been left to chance,' he said. 'That is why we have triumphed so consistently. For so long. I was there beside him in the beerhall, you know? I marched with the Führer through the streets of Munich in '23. How many are left who can say that? Ah, Schilte, you should have heard him that night!'

'A defining moment, Gauleiter.'

'The turning point, Schilte. He made it so clear to everyone that night. His words turned them inside out. Yes, the way you would turn a glove inside out. From that moment I knew victory was inevitable. In that moment I knew what a true leader could achieve. And in the years that followed! What achievements! What enduring glory! They will find it hard to forget us. And now . . . ' Müller wrinkled his upper lip where the spirit-gum and moustache had begun to sting.

'And now you're going home,' said the actor.

'Quite so,' said Müller. 'The spectacles?'

'Forgive me.'

Connors handed him the spectacles and Müller slipped them on. He turned to the right and to the left and nodded approvingly at the face in the mirror. 'You have excelled yourself, Mr Connors.'

'They won't recognize you when you step off the plane in Berlin.'

Müller stood up and Schilte held out the raincoat for him to put on. '*Sagen Sie es dem Dummkopf, Schilte,*' he said. '*Ich will seinen Gesichtsausdruck sehen.*'

'*Mit Vergnügen, Gauleiter.*'

'I suppose,' said Connors, gathering the make-up sticks into the box, 'I'd better polish up my German double-damned quick.'

'That will not be necessary, Mr Connors.'

'Come now, Herr Schilte, it's only good manners to make an attempt speak your host's language.'

'But Germany is not our destination, Mr Connors.'

Connors looked up. 'Not Germany?' he said. 'I don't understand. I thought the plan was . . . '

'We are flying west, Mr Connors—not east.'

'West?'

'And then a discreet and leisurely sea-voyage all the way to . . . well, that need not concern you.'

'You're running away?'

'Nothing so ignoble. We live to fight another day. That is our duty.'

'The Careys too?'

'The Careys?' The Gauleiter was buttoning his raincoat. 'You are being unusually naive, Mr Connors.'

'Ah, I see. And what about me?'

'You have not been forgotten.'

Connors looked up and saw Schilte's raised arm reflected in the mirror. Then the leather cosh came down on the back of his head. And everything went black.

Stay in your room. I may need to find you. Those were Connors's instructions.

Which was all very well and orders were orders but Frank seemed to have been sitting there for hours. What could Connors be up to? And why had those dogs started barking? He couldn't see anything from the window. It was still raining heavily. Surely Connors didn't really expect him just to sit there and do nothing?

He got up and went across to the door.

The handle turned but the door wouldn't open. It was locked.

Simon Carey threw himself into the armchair.

'Can't say I enjoyed that much,' he said.

'The dogs will be perfectly happy in the stables,' said his

122

father. 'Someone's bound to hear them eventually and let them out.'

'Poor, loyal creatures,' said Rowena.

The Careys and Mrs Cato had gathered in the drawing room. They were dressed for the journey. Restricted to one suitcase each, they had put on as many clothes as possible and all looked several sizes larger. Their luggage was piled by the door. And time was passing heavily. The grandfather clock which stood between the windows seemed to tick ever more slowly and ever more loudly.

'I'll tell you what,' said Hugh. 'Why don't we have a last glass of champagne together?'

'What a lovely idea, Hugh.'

'Shall I go down to the cellar, sir?' said Mrs Cato.

'No, Mrs Cato. I'll go. You get out the glasses. And bring one for Felicity. I think this occasion is special enough for that—don't you, darling?' He smiled at his daughter. But Felicity didn't answer. 'Simon?' he said.

'Father?'

'Go up and ask the Gauleiter and Herr Schilte to join us, will you?'

'Certainly, father.'

'Hugh?' Rowena Carey followed her husband to the door. 'Have you spoken to Schilte?' she said quietly. 'About the boy?'

'Yes, my dear,' he said hurriedly.

'Good. Well? What about that champagne?'

Simon took the stairs two at a time.

What an opportunity! To be able to speak to the Gauleiter alone. He'd obviously made a bit of an impression last night with all that blood stuff. Now would be his chance to let Herr Müller see what sort of a chap he really was. To tell him his plans. To tell him what he was going to do when they got to Germany.

Simon was surprised to find that the door to the Gauleiter's room was ajar. But there was no answer when

123

he knocked. He hesitated for a moment; then pushed at it gently.

The Gauleiter was obviously still packing. There was a suitcase open on the bed and clothes thrown everywhere. And someone seemed to have spilled a box of face-powder on the counterpane, the sort of thing he'd often seen on his mother's dressing-table. That struck him as rather odd. And there were also what looked like five or six lipsticks crushed into the carpet. But no sign of the Gauleiter. He was about to go out again when he caught sight of Müller's uniform hanging from the picture-rail. It was, he thought, still one of the most beautiful things he'd ever seen.

He went over to it and touched it reverently with the tips of his fingers. As he did so there was a splintering crash. Simon spun round. The door of the wardrobe burst open and Douglas Connors stumbled out.

Simon stared. 'You?' he said. 'What are you doing here?'

'Getting out, you oaf,' Connors replied, shaking the cord from his wrists. 'And you'll do the same if you've any sense.'

'But . . . but where's the Gauleiter? And Herr Schilte?'

'They've flown the coop, dear boy. You and your delightful family have been sold down the Swanee.'

As he spoke there was the sound of gunfire from somewhere outside. Connors ran across to the window. 'How very dramatic. And bang on cue!' he said. 'I think you've got more visitors, Simon. Do thank your mother for me. It's been such a pleasure.'

'But what about . . . what shall I tell . . . ?'

But Douglas Connors was already through the door

Chapter 14

The dogs were barking frantically now. And that was gunfire.

Frank looked desperately round the room and his eye fell on Simon's cricket-bat. Perfect. He grabbed it and began smashing at the panelled door. The wood splintered and he was able to reach through to the other side. Whoever had locked him in had left the key in the lock. He turned it and pulled the door open.

He ran up the stairs and along the landing. He pushed open Felicity's door and crossed her room into Nanny Gale's.

He was pulling aside the shutters when a noise made him turn. Connors was standing in the doorway. He had Simon Carey's shotgun under his arm.

'Two minds with but a single thought,' said the actor.

'This way,' said Frank, and began to clamber out.

'We must keep our heads. And stay away from the windows!'

Hugh Carey shepherded his wife and Mrs Cato back against the wall.

'Felicity! Come here,' he called. 'Felicity!'

And Felicity Carey, looking utterly bewildered, walked slowly across the room as splinters of glass fell around her.

At which point the door burst open and Simon ran in.

'Simon, get down!' his father called. 'They're shooting at the windows. Where's the Gauleiter?'

'He's gone.'

'What are you talking about?'

'Schilte's gone too. Mother, they've both gone!'

Hugh and Rowena Carey looked at each other.

'Nonsense, Simon,' she said. 'They can't have.'

'They've done a bunk. The actor told me.'

There was barking out in the hall and the dogs came crashing in and threw themselves on the Careys, licking their faces and pawing at their coats.

'I'm going to fetch the shotgun,' said Simon, pushing the dogs away.

'Simon, wait!' his father called.

But just as Simon reached the door two figures appeared there: a young woman and a tall young man in an RAF greatcoat. They both held pistols in their hands.

'Stay where you are,' said the young woman. Simon immediately made to move. 'I shan't hesitate to shoot,' she said. 'And I shall shoot to kill.'

'Müller?' said the young man. 'Where is he? Please don't waste our time. We know he's here.'

Rowena Carey stood up. 'Get out of my house,' she said imperiously.

'Rowena . . . '

'Be quiet, Hugh! Well? Did you hear me, young woman? How dare you walk into my home like this! Who the hell do you think you are?'

Gwen signalled and two men with rifles came in from the hallway. 'Take these people outside,' she said. 'You know what to do with them.'

'What? Wait!' Hugh stepped forward and put his arm round his daughter's shoulder. 'Wait. You can't shoot us. You can't. Not just like that. At least let the children . . . '

Gwen Wood looked at him contemptuously. 'You've been keeping company with your Nazi pals too long, Mr Carey,' she said. 'We're not going to shoot you. That isn't the way we do things. Outside, please.'

The Careys and Mrs Cato were hustled into the hall, which was full of partisans, and on to the front steps where they were met by Alec, Mervyn, and Les.

'Well?' said Alec.

'Wings' shook his head. 'They've said nothing,' he said.

'You're harbouring a murderer, Carey,' said Alec. 'I want him. Where's Müller?'

'Look here, I don't know,' said Hugh Carey desperately. 'I really have no idea; I swear.'

'You're lying.'

'He's gone!' Mrs Cato stepped away from the others. 'He's gone and you'll never find him,' she said triumphantly. 'You won't catch him now. He's too clever for the likes of you. Men like him always are.'

'Mrs Cato!'

'Don't pay them any heed, Mr Hugh—they're dirt, the whole pack of them. And in time they'll be crushed under the heel and kicked back into the gutter where they belong.' And she threw up her arm: 'Heil Hitler! Sieg Heil! Heil Hitler!'

One of the partisans released the bolt on his rifle but Alec held up his hand. 'She's not worth the bullet,' he said. 'Is this true, Carey? Has he gone?'

'Hugh, don't tell them!'

'Think of the children, Rowena. Yes,' he said. 'Yes, he's gone. And I really have no idea where.'

'When?'

'A quarter of an hour ago. Maybe less. He didn't exactly announce his departure.'

Alec pulled a map from his pocket. '"Wings", look here, I've ringed three places I thought a plane could land.'

'There,' said 'Wings', 'that's the only place they can try.'

'Right. We'll leave the Winscombe men to secure these people and the house. The rest of you come with me.'

And they set off down the steps towards where the police car was waiting.

Frank was first to drop onto the roof of the shed; and from there he slipped down quickly into the stableyard. Connors came scrambling after him.

'You're rather good at this, Eric, aren't you?' he said. 'Now what?'

'Follow me.'

The actor hesitated but then hurried after him.

As they came round the corner of the house they saw the Careys under guard on the steps and the partisans making for the car.

Frank stopped and waved frantically. 'Don't shoot,' he called, 'Don't shoot!'

The partisans and the Careys all turned to look in his direction.

And Frank was about to run forward to join them when he felt fingers gripping his collar. 'You really shouldn't have done that,' said Connors, placing the barrel of the shotgun against Frank's cheek.

'Good God,' said Alec. 'That's . . . '

'Frank? It is! It is! Frank!' yelled Les. 'I was right. I knew I was right. Frank?'

'Keep your distance!' Connors called. 'All of you! And keep away from that car. I shan't hesitate to shoot.' He turned to Frank: 'Now, what you're going to do is behave sensibly and walk very slowly to where that police car is parked. Do you understand? Don't do anything silly. I really have very little to lose.'

'But what are you doing?' said Frank. 'They're the partisans. They're on our side.'

'That's just the problem, dear boy.'

'What?'

Connors pushed Frank forwards. 'Just start walking!'

'You . . . You're with the Nazis!' said Frank. 'That's it, isn't it? And the Careys. You're with them.'

'D'you know,' said Connors, 'I think the sad thing is I'm not really with either of them.'

'And it was you, wasn't it? It was you betrayed "Uncle" Herbert Sillitoe.'

'Just do as you're told. And keep moving.'

Les and Alec watched helplessly as the two figures made their way towards the car.

'What can we do, Mr Thrale?'

'Not a lot at the minute.'

'Oh, yes there is.' Les reached into his jacket and took out his Luger.

'No, Les,' said Alec. 'You'll hit Frank.'

'But, Mr Thrale . . . '

On the steps Hugh Carey gripped his daughter's shoulder as they watched Connors and Frank stumble towards the police car. 'Go on, man,' he whispered. 'If Connors can commandeer that car we stand a chance!'

When Frank and Connors arrived at the car Connors's grip tightened on Frank's collar. 'Open the driver's door,' he said. 'Do it slowly. No tricks. I'm warning you.'

Frank reached for the handle. But as he did so the rear door flew open. It caught Connors hard on the thigh and threw him sideways.

In a flash Les dropped to one knee, levelling the Luger. His bandaged right hand was forcing him to shoot with his left and the pistol shook unsteadily as he took aim.

Connors was stumbling to his feet, struggling to bring the shotgun to bear on Frank who was backing away from him.

On the steps of the house Felicity Carey shook herself free of her father's hand.

'Felicity!' he hissed. 'What are you doing?'

But she took only one step down onto the gravel of the driveway. And then stood very still. She closed her eyes and rammed her hand into the pocket of her raincoat.

There was the sound of a single shot. It echoed off the front of the house and died quickly away.

Felicity Winfred Carey slowly opened her eyes. She saw Connors frown. A look of irritation passed across his handsome face. No more than that. Then the shotgun fell from his fingers and clattered onto the gravel. And the actor slid down slowly beside it.

'Frank!' Les jumped up and ran forward.

Alec and the others hurried to where Connors lay. And Gwen reached into the back seat and helped Bill Tate up.

129

'God Almighty, Bill, you saved the day,' she said.

'I couldn't see what was happening,' he said, struggling for breath. 'But I knew he must be up to no good. I just kicked at the door as hard as I could.'

'Are you all right? Bill?'

But Bill Tate was staring uncomprehendingly in the direction of the two boys who were laughing and shaking hands a few feet away.

'Bill?'

'No,' he said quietly, shaking his head. 'No, that'd be too much to ask. Frank? Frank?'

Frank turned.

'Frank? Is that you?'

Frank hesitated and then walked slowly towards the figure hunched on the back seat of the car. 'Dad?' he said quietly.

'Hullo, old son.'

'Dad, is that you?'

'Not before time, eh?'

'But . . . '

Bill reached out his hand and Frank shook it awkwardly. 'Dad . . . '

'I'd say we've got a bit of catching up to do, wouldn't you?'

But Alec Thrale was pulling open the driver's door and urging 'Wings' inside. 'We've got to move,' he said. 'Fast.'

'Oh, Alec, be fair. It's his father.'

'We're going to lose Müller, Gwen.' Alec turned to Frank and Bill. 'I'm sorry. You two can stay, if you like. But we may have missed him already.'

'Müller's got away?' said Bill.

Alec nodded.

'Let's get after him, then. Come on, Frank. Get in beside me.'

Frank slid in beside his father. And Les piled in next to them. Gwen and Mervyn jumped onto the running boards and they screeched out of the drive.

'Here,' said Alec, stabbing at the map with his finger, as

they bucketed along the narrow lane making for the Downs. 'It's the only possible place.'

'It is. But blessed if I'd care to land there,' said 'Wings' doubtfully. 'And taking off again would be a nightmare.'

'It's got to be the place.'

They came to a crossroads and Alec signalled for them to stop. 'Wings' pulled up and turned off the engine. In the silence Alec got out and stood looking up at the clouds.

'There! I can hear it,' he said. 'Over there! Look! There it is!' Away to the left, low in the sky, was a small plane. Alec jumped back into the car. 'Up this lane. Quickly! Quickly! Shift, "Wings"! We're going to lose him otherwise.'

Schilte came hurrying back to where Müller was waiting under the trees.

'It's here,' he said. 'We must get aboard the moment it comes to a halt.'

'Didn't I tell you this English rain would not deter them, Schilte?'

They walked quickly to the edge of the long field below the Downs. Out of the sky to the east, the light aeroplane swooped, hung for a moment, and began to glide towards them. It bounced once or twice as it ran along the grass. Then, with the engines still running, it turned back into the wind. The pilot threw open his cockpit window and waved as the two men ran across to the door in the fuselage which was already opening.

Schilte handed Müller up and then climbed aboard himself.

The door was pulled into place, the engines whined to pitch, and they set off back along the grass.

Müller shook the hand the co-pilot offered him. 'Heroic,' he said breathlessly.

'And with no time to spare,' said Schilte, looking back through the window to where the partisans' police car was pulling up at the edge of the field.

'Meticulous planning, Schilte,' said Müller exultantly. 'As always!'

And they began to laugh as they felt the aircraft lift and start into the air.

The partisans stumbled from the car. They saw the plane gain height and then drop back to earth and continue its effort to take off.

'That pilot's as good as they come!' said 'Wings' grudgingly.

Alec Thrale grabbed his rifle from the seat beside him. He wrapped the leather carrying-strap tightly round his arm, leaned forward and braced himself against the roof of the car. The aircraft was gathering speed. He held his breath. And squeezed the trigger. They saw the coping of the cockpit shatter. But the plane kept on going and, with a final skip, it lifted into the air and began to climb towards the crest of the hill.

Alec brought his fist down angrily. 'We've lost him!'

They watched the wings of the plane seesaw in a final contemptuous salute.

'Unfair! Bloody well unfair,' yelled Mervyn, shaking his fist at the heavens.

And, as he did, the fuselage seemed to shiver from one end to the other. The engine began to splutter and the plane began to lose height. The partisans looked at each other and rushed forward as, in one terrible, swooping turn, the plane rolled on to its back and plunged nose-first into the hill. There was a roar, black smoke, and a pillar of flame.

In the silence that followed, the smoke drifted raggedly in the falling rain. All that remained of the plane, its passengers and crew, was a scattering of twisted metal and a dark smudge on the ancient chalk.

Chapter 15

Frank sat by the window watching his father sleep. He always seemed to sleep so badly: turning this way and that and racked by long bouts of coughing.

In the days since the arrest of the Careys and Müller's death Frank and his dad had been inseparable. They had talked non-stop. Or, at least, Frank had. He had told his father everything: about Seabourne and Shevington; about Nan dying—that had been the hardest thing; about his years with the Resistance; and about being captured by the Careys. And his father seemed content to listen and occasionally pat his son's hand. But of his own life during their time apart Bill Tate said very little. Best forgotten, son, he'd told him. That's over and done with. What's important is we're together again.

The partisans had transferred their HQ to Winscombe Court and were now waiting for orders.

What should they do next? Disband? Or make their way east to where the last fighting regiments of the Wehrmacht were trapped on the coast and fenlands of Lincolnshire and Norfolk?

Finally, when they had been there almost a week, news came of the American landings: amphibious assaults along the South Coast and paratroop drops on Salisbury Plain. The liberators seemed to have met with little resistance. To all intents and purposes the invaders had gone.

But still no orders came. And still the partisans waited.

Was it really over? There was a bewildering sense of normality everywhere. And no one knew quite what to do about it. Even the weather had taken a turn for the better.

There were signs of early spring all down the valley. Most mornings 'Wings' could be found with a book in his hand sitting in a wicker chair on the terrace where Gwen would join him from time to time. They would sit together, reading or chatting quietly. Mervyn had set up his armoury in the stables and spent his time tirelessly replenishing his fuses and explosives. Les spent a lot of time watching him and Alec pottered about the gardens and grounds. The Careys' dogs had taken a great liking to him. The Careys themselves remained confined and under guard in a room in the East Wing.

'Frank?'

Frank looked up as the door opened. It was Les.

'All right to come in?'

'Yes. Dad's asleep.'

'I've got something for you.'

'My hat! Les, you found my trilby!'

'Yes, I went out this morning and fetched it in.'

'Thanks, Les! I've missed that hat. Silly, en't it—but I have.'

'It was your lucky hat.'

'It's been that, all right!' There was an awkward silence. 'How's the hand?' said Frank.

'Better,' said Les. 'Much better.' He wriggled his fingers. 'See? Gwen says it'll be right as rain in a day or two.'

'I'll still never know how you managed that shot with your hand like that?'

'Cos I had to,' said Les. 'It's as simple as that. Listen, I'm going up on the roof. I wondered if you wanted to come?'

Frank looked back at his dad who seemed to be sleeping quietly at last. 'Yes, course!'

They went up through the attics together and out onto the windswept leads.

'So how're you doing?' said Les, as they stood by the parapet. 'I ain't hardly seen you at all since . . . well, since everything happened.'

'I know. I've had no time what with looking after Dad

and everything. What about you? Are you getting used to it? You know, all the peace and quiet?'

'Nah! Don't seem right, do it? Everything coming to a stop like this. What about you?'

'Me? I s'pose I'm getting used to it,' said Frank. And added after a moment: 'No, I'm not, Les, I ain't . . . not really.'

'What's up?'

'I wouldn't tell this to anyone else, Les . . . Fact is, it's not the peace and quiet I can't get used to . . . '

'How d'you mean?'

'Les, I don't know who he is,' Frank said quietly.

'Who?'

'Dad. Les, I didn't recognize him first off. I didn't know it was him. He's not the same.'

'We ain't none of us the same, Frank.'

'But he's not . . . he's not how I remember him, Les; and he isn't . . . he isn't what I expected him to be . . . you know, when I did find him. All the time I was looking for him and . . . I don't know where I am, Les.'

They stood together silently, staring down the valley to the village and the White Horse far beyond.

'Mervyn's a cunning old bird, you know,' said Les, nodding towards the distant hillside. 'It was his idea to uncover the White Horse.'

'Was it?' Frank reached up and pulled his trilby a little tighter to his head. 'I was up here with Simon Carey looking at it the day I lost my hat.'

'Was you?' said Les. 'I knew it was your hat, you know. The minute I saw it. Course, nobody would believe me. Can't blame them, I s'pose. You know, thinking as how you was . . . '

'Sorry, Les.'

'What?' Les laughed. 'What're you apologizing for?'

'You thinking I was dead all that time.'

'That's you all over, Frank Tate. Apologizin' for a thing like that.'

'What're you going to do now?'

'Me? I'm pushing on. There's still a few of 'em left who need sorting out. And you?'

'Me and Dad's going back to Shevington.' Frank waited. But Les didn't respond. 'Les?' he said.

'I heard you.'

'You could come with us, you know.'

'Nah.'

'Of course you could. Les, it's where you belong.'

'Leave it, Frank.' Les started back towards the ladder. 'They'll be collecting the prisoners,' he said. 'I've got to be down there to keep an eye on the locals. Some of 'em's a bit trigger-happy and they ain't too fond of Mr and Mrs "High-and-Mighty" Carey.'

'Collecting the Careys?' Frank hurried after him. 'How d'you mean?'

'They're being taken to Charborough. There's a lorry coming for 'em.'

'Les, I've got to speak to Felicity before they take her away.'

'The girl? You'll have to be quick, then. Come on!'

On the gravel drive outside the front door the Careys and Mrs Cato were waiting to be loaded into the back of an open lorry. They stood beside their suitcases looking dishevelled and tired. Simon was already climbing aboard.

'Felicity?' called Frank, as he and Les came down the steps of the house. And Felicity looked round and started towards him. One of the guards tried to stop her but Les signalled to let her through.

'I so hoped you'd come, Eric,' she said.

'I would have come to see you before but my dad's not well and . . . well, everything else, you know.'

'I'm glad you found your father. Did you know we're going away now?' she said. 'I don't know where.'

'You mustn't worry. You'll be all right,' he said. 'I see you've still got your book with you.'

'Yes,' she said. 'And now you can see how true it is, can't you? You know, about things not always having to turn out to be horrible.'

'Well, there you are. What with that and that wish you've still got to use up, you're bound to be all right.'

'I haven't got the wish any more, Eric,' she said.

'Have you made it then? What was your wish? Not to be taken to Germany? Was that it?'

'No,' she said, 'it wasn't that. May I whisper?'

He leaned down and she whispered in his ear.

'Felicity . . . '

She took his hand, placed something in his palm and closed his fingers round it.

'You won't forget me, will you?' she said.

'I en't got all day,' said the guard. 'I've got to get this lorry back to Charborough.'

'Goodbye, Eric.'

'Look,' he said, 'it's Frank. My real name's Frank.'

'That doesn't matter. Goodbye, Eric.'

And she ran across to the lorry and was pulled up into it. The guard clambered up behind her, secured the tailboard, and the lorry drove away down the drive.

'What was all that about?' said Les.

Frank opened his fingers and showed his friend the fragment of bone she had placed in the palm of his hand.

'What is it?'

'It's half a wishbone. Les, when you shot Connors—did you really think you were going to hit him?'

'True bill?' Les shook his head. 'No, can't say I did. It was a million to one chance, Frank. But I had to try. He'd have shot you otherwise.'

'I reckon he would. Les, that's what she wished for.'

'Do what?'

'That was her wish, Les—that you'd get him before he got me.'

''Struth! Then . . . '

They turned and looked down the drive. But the lorry and its prisoners was already a cloud of dust and had disappeared through the gates of Winscombe Court.

★ ★ ★

It was as lunch was almost over later that day when Alec Thrale cleared his throat and asked if he might have their attention for a minute or two.

They always ate together round the big table in the Carey's dining room. Drawn to it from whatever activity they found themselves doing or wherever they found themselves. Seeking each other's company.

'I wanted to tell you officially,' said Alec, 'I've had word from the Committee. We're being disbanded.'

'Just like that?' said Mervyn angrily.

'Apparently the Americans don't want us interfering. However, there's an opportunity for any of you who do want to fight on to join up with units in the east. There'll be fighting there for a while, I daresay. That's a choice for you to make. And you've a day or two to do your considerin'. There'll be a truck coming through to take anyone east as wants to go.'

'We're coming with you, chief,' said Mervyn.

'No, Mervyn,' he said. 'Not this time. I'm not going, you see.'

'How d'you mean?'

'I'm not going, cos I'm going home.' Alec held up his hand. 'I'm going home. That's the reason I fought the Jerries in the first place—so there'd be a home to go home to. And now we've beat them that's where I'm going . . . in the hope that there is. I don't, I can't and wouldn't, insist you do the same. You must all do what's best for you. That's for you to decide. I'm not in charge any more.' He smiled. 'Not that I ever was. I've never known a bunch of people so opinionated. No,' he added, 'nor any so brave.' No one spoke or looked at one another. It wasn't a moment they'd ever considered would come. And here it was. Awkward and embarrassing. There was a silence as each one of them sat staring at the table waiting. 'We've lived with each other's lives in our hands for a long time,' said Alec. 'It seems like a lifetime. I could not have asked for truer companions. And I shan't meet your like again. I hope you find happy lives and that they are long and without shadows. And . . . I shall never forget you.'

And before anyone could reply he got up and went out.

It was early the following morning when Alec and Les walked down the drive of Winscombe Court together. They stopped when they reached the gate.

'You'll not come with me?' the keeper asked.

Les shook his head. 'No, Mr Thrale.'

'Very well. You're grown man enough to make your own decisions, that I do know. But you're wrong, Leslie.' And Alec held out his hand. 'Take care of yourself.'

'Thanks, Mr Thrale,' said Les. 'For all of it.'

'Alec, Leslie. It's about time you started calling me Alec, don't you think? Good luck to you.' And Alec Thrale turned and set off down the road.

'Mr Thrale?' Les called. 'Alec?'

'Yes?'

'Remember me to . . . you know, to everybody.'

'I'll do that, Leslie.'

'Has he gone?' Frank asked when Les came back to the house.

Les nodded.

'But not you, eh?'

'There's nothing in Shevington for me, Frank. Not no more. I'm going with Mervyn. To finish the job.'

'What about Gwen and "Wings"?'

'They're going to Shropshire. That's where she comes from. To see if her farm's still there. What about you?'

'Me and Dad'll be heading for Shevington ourselves in a week or so.'

Les sat down on the steps. 'Everybody's saying cheerio, ain't they?' he said glumly. 'I thought the end of it would be different to this. Sort of . . . noisier, you know. A proper battle and . . . you know what I mean. I thought I'd feel like we'd won.'

'None of it's the way we thought it would be, is it?' said Frank. 'Come in and talk to Dad.'

'Frank?' said Les as they went back inside.

'What?'

'When I shot that Connors . . . '

'What about it?'

'I wasn't just paying my debt, you know? You know, cos you saved my life that other time. It wasn't just that. You're my best pal. Always will be.'

'Likewise, Les Gill.'

Homecomings . . . (April/May 1945)

Alec Thrale came down quickly through the woods above
Shevington Hall. The undergrowth was thick and the paths
neglected but he knew them blindfold. He had walked them
all his life.

He stepped from the trees and stood looking across at
the house and the destruction piled on the lawns around
it. The walls of the Hall were dark with soot and one wing
was a hollow shell of blackened brick. The sight of so much
devastation struck him less painfully than he expected. He
had seen too many ruins in the last three years, too many
burnt-out shells of men and buildings.

A group of villagers had gathered near the foot of the
steps. As Alec approached they fell silent. It was Mr
Dearman, the man who ran the village shop, who came
across to where he stood: 'Alec?' he said uncertainly. 'Is
that you?'

Alec nodded.

'Well, I'm blessed! Welcome! Welcome home,' he said
and shook the keeper's hand.

'What happened here?'

'The Yanks bombed it. The day after the Germans left.
Ironic, isn't it? Still, I suppose they couldn't afford to take
any chances.'

Alec walked up the steps and into the entrance hall. The
marble floor was stained with soot and strewn with charred
documents.

An American soldier with a rifle slung from his shoulder appeared on one of the landings above and called to
him:

141

'Can't you read, pal? There's a sign on the door: Keep Out.'

'I saw it,' said Alec evenly. 'I used to work here. Well,' he gestured towards the door, 'out there at any rate.'

'Is that so?' said the soldier.

Alec nodded. 'Still,' he said, 'I don't suppose you've much call for a gamekeeper at the moment.'

'For a what?'

It took him ten minutes to walk home to Keeper's Cottage. He went in through the kitchen door and waited quietly on the familiar flagstones. Almost at once there was the sound of footsteps in the passage and he heard his wife's voice:

'Mildred, dear? Is that you, Mildred?'

When she saw him Vera Thrale stopped in the doorway. 'Alec?' she said.

'Hello, Vera.'

'Oh, Alec,' she replied. 'I knew it . . . I knew you'd come.'

'Here I am.'

'You are, Alec—you are.'

And she stepped forward and took his hand. And looked up into his face.

But Alec Thrale could not see her. His eyes were filled with tears.

'Hello, Mr Thrale?'

He brushed a hand across his cheek and turned to look at the young woman who had come in from the yard. 'Mildred? Mildred, dear girl!' he said. 'You too. You're safe—the both of you.'

Mill nodded. 'Is Les with you, Mr Thrale?' she said.

'No, my dear . . . no, I'm afraid he isn't.'

'Is he dead?'

'No, Mildred,' he said quickly. 'No, he's not dead.'

She smiled. 'I'm glad. And is he going to . . . ? Well,' she said quickly, 'it don't matter. I'm everso glad you're all right, Mr Thrale. Everso glad.'

And she turned and walked back out into the yard.

Germany, late April 1945

The remains of the town were silhouetted starkly against the glow of the setting sun; and from the ruins charred beams and rafters reached up to clutch at the sky like the fingers of a blackened corpse.

The tyres of countless lorries, the wheels of farm-carts and wagons, the passage of tank tracks and weary feet had churned the road to a quagmire. There were abandoned vehicles as far as the eye could see: mud-splattered, their doors thrown open, they stood like islands in the river of people flowing west. West. Away from the advancing Red Army and towards the American lines. Men, women, and children. A flood of faces moving slowly by, pale and blank with exhaustion or dark and anxious with fear, looking up constantly at the lowering sky. What possessions the fugitives had managed to salvage were piled onto handcarts, into bulging suitcases, crammed into bags or clasped tightly in their arms. The roadside was littered with discarded belongings. One bundle, fashioned from an old sheet, had burst open and its contents lay scattered in the mud: some letters; an empty jewel-box; a saucepan; and an ornately carved, wooden cuckoo clock.

General von Schreier and Oberleutnant Lang stood beside their staff-car and watched the crowd press past. Most of those who passed didn't spare them a glance. But one old man spat as he went by.

'Shall we go on, Herr General?' Lang said quietly.

'On, Werner?'

'I can syphon fuel from one of these abandoned vehicles.'

'I don't think so.' The general extinguished his cigarette. 'We have come to the end of the road.'

'What do you mean?'

'It's finished, Werner. Destroy your identity papers. And discard that uniform as quickly as you can.'

'But, Herr General . . . '

'If you do that there may be a chance for you.'

'I am not looking for such a chance, Herr General.'

'Someone must reclaim our honour, Werner. Someone must rebuild all this.'

'There is still fighting around Berlin. I am coming with you.'

'No. I am going alone.' Von Schreier smiled. 'These are the last orders I will ever give you, Oberleutnant Lang. Please do me the courtesy of obeying them.' The general offered his hand. 'Goodbye, my friend.'

The two men shook hands and Werner Lang watched von Schreier turn and push away through the oncoming refugees. He watched until the general was lost from sight and then he turned and started in the opposite direction.

Not long after, two boys who had been foraging in a ruined house along the Berlin road, came across the general sitting against the blackened wall of what had once been someone's kitchen. He had shot himself. They quarrelled over who should have the pistol and then rummaged through his pockets. To their delight they found a few loose squares of chocolate and a packet of cigarettes which was almost full. They also found a piece of paper with scribbles of what looked like trees and animals on it—were they sheep? They wrapped the chocolate in it. And moved on to the next house.

On an afternoon some weeks later two figures were making their way up the lane from Shevington village.

When they reached the bend and Nan Tate's cottage came in sight Bill Tate stopped and leaned on his son's shoulder.

'We're home, Frank,' he said.

Frank smiled. 'I used to dream about this,' he said.

'Did you?'

'A lot. I'd be waiting by the gate and you'd be coming up the lane. You used to call out to me when you got to about here. That's how I used to dream it.'

144

'And here we are doing it together.'

Frank looked at his dad and nodded. 'Yes,' he said. 'That's the important thing.'

'But nobody waiting,' said Bill hoarsely. 'No. No Nan watching out for us. Rest her soul. But I dare swear she ain't far away. Nor ever will be. Come on, old son.'

They pushed open the gate and walked round to the overgrown garden at the back. There was a pram standing under the kitchen window.

'I used to help her collect the eggs,' said Frank, pointing to where Nan Tate's chicken-run had once stood.

His dad smiled. 'So did I.'

A face appeared briefly at the window and almost at once a man came out of the back door carrying a poker. 'Get off out of it! Did you hear me?' he called. 'Go on! We've got ways with vagrants round here.'

'Not much of a welcome,' said Bill.

'That's Edie's husband,' said Frank. 'That's Len Worth.'

'I know. Hello, brother-in-law.'

'Do what?' Len Worth frowned and came closer. 'What's going on? Good God, is that you, boy?' he said.

'Yes. And this is my dad.'

'Well, I'm damned. So it is. Edie? Edie?'

Edie Worth came hurrying out of the kitchen and Rose and the baby were with her. 'Len, whatever, is it? What's the matter?' she asked.

'Look here, Edie. It's your brother. And that son of his.'

'Frank?' Edie put her hands up to her face. 'Oh my Lord! And Bill? Bill, it's never you, is it?'

''Fraid so, sister mine,' he said.

'Is it really you, Bill? Look at you! Oh, Bill, what have they done to you?'

And Edie began to cry.

For a moment they all stood very still, like the awkward figures in a family photograph. Then Rose ran to Frank and hugged him. And Edie took her brother's hand.

And Colin Worth came careering out of the house.

'Listen, everybody! Listen!' he called. 'You won't believe

it! Guess what? It's on the wireless. Oh, hello, Frank!' he said casually, grinning at his cousin. 'Listen, listen all of you. It's just been on the news. He's dead! He's dead! Hitler's dead.'

VE Day, 8 May 1945

'Nice morning for it,' someone called, as the Worths, with Rose, Phil, and the baby, came out of the bus station and turned into Kilgarriff Street.

And several voices replied: 'That it is!' And it was. A sparkling spring morning without a cloud in the sky.

The bus station in Seabourne and the streets nearby thronged with people who had travelled in for the Victory Parade. Seabourne had been one of the first places where the Nazis had stormed ashore; and now, four long years later, the small seaside town was celebrating the defeat of the invader throughout Europe. Red, white, and blue bunting was strung across the streets; Union Jacks had been taken from their hiding places and fluttered in the breeze; and every shop window displayed newspaper photographs of victorious generals.

When they reached the High Street the Shevington contingent were forced to wait with everyone else while sections of the parade formed up in the roadway.

'Where's our Bill got to?' asked Edie, looking up and down the pavement.

'Gone off with that boy of his,' her husband replied. 'Too fond of their own company to bother with the likes of us.'

'I expect they've gone to look at that place where they used to live,' said Edie. 'We'll meet up again later, I daresay.'

'Look at that!' Len pointed to the group where the mayor in his robes, his wife, his mace-bearer, and staff from the Town Hall were lined up waiting their turn to move off down to the Promenade. 'You tell me what right people like that have got to be marching on a day like this?' he said loudly. 'Eh? You tell me that. It's people like me as should be marching today. Men who've suffered for their country.'

'Oh, be quiet, Dad,' said Rose. 'People are looking at you. Give me the baby, Phil.'

'I can manage,' her husband replied. But Phil's arm had still not recovered from the bullet he'd taken through his shoulder that day at the Hall.

'No, you can't,' she said. 'Let me have him. I want to hold him up to watch. I want him to see everything today so's he'll remember it all. Eh, George? You'll remember this the rest of your life, won't you?' And George Gingell opened his eyes and smiled. At least, Rose and Edie said that he did.

'Come on,' said Len, 'lively! We want to get a decent position down on the Prom.'

And they hurried across the road with the rest.

'Just let me catch my breath, Frank.'

Frank and Bill Tate stopped by the railings overlooking the beach. On the pebbles below children were playing among the tank-traps and one or two families had spread tablecloths and were eating sandwiches. The sea was hardly moving. There was just breeze enough to ripple the edge of the water where it washed quietly along the tideline. In the bay beyond there were several fishing-boats, a solitary yacht, and a Motor Torpedo Boat whose deck was busy with sailors.

'Looks better without the barbed-wire, doesn't it?' said Bill. 'Remember how we used to walk here of an evening?'

Frank nodded. 'Remember that soldier we used to talk to—Yorkie? It was him who told me he'd seen you and . . . '

But Bill had a sudden fit of coughing which doubled him up and left him clutching the railings.

Frank waited. He was used to it now. To the coughing.

And everything else. Bill's hair had grown and he'd regained a little of the weight he'd lost. About the face especially. He had begun to look like the man who had been his father. That had really been the worst thing, Frank realized that now, the way his dad had looked. Not who he was. He was the same man he'd always been. The man with half a sandwich in his sandwich box. Yes, he was getting used to his dad.

'Is he OK?' The young man in the American uniform stopped beside them. 'Anythin' I can do?'

Frank shook his head. 'Thanks all the same.'

'Grand day, though!' He didn't look more than a year or two older than Frank, neat and clean in his freshly-pressed uniform. 'Historic too, I guess. And I'm gonna be able to tell them I was here. Yessir! Victory-Europe Day in little old Britain. Do you care for gum?' He drew a packet of chewing-gum from his pocket and passed it to Frank. He winked. 'Girls go crazy for it,' he said. 'Listen, are you sure I can't do anything to help?'

'We'll manage,' said Frank. 'But thanks for asking.'

The young man shrugged. 'OK. See you sometime.' And with a wave he sauntered away along the Prom.

'All right, Dad?'

Bill nodded. 'Yes. Let's go, eh? I'd like to have a look at the old place before the parade gets started properly. Come on.'

'You sure you're all right?' said Frank, after they'd walked along in silence for a minute or two.

'Me? Yes. Sorry, old son,' said Bill, 'I was miles away. Just thinking of young Gwen and "Wings". You know, wondering how they're getting on. And that Welshman. Just wondering about them all. Good people. Though it ain't likely we'll ever meet again, is it? I suppose that's what happens in wartime, eh? People meet each other, stop for a bit of a chat, and then move on . . . one way or another.'

'It's Les I've been thinking about,' said Frank.

'I reckon Les has got to come to his own conclusions, Frank. He ain't a lad to let someone make up his mind for him, you know that. I could see that even in the short time we was with him. Les had to go his own way. God Almighty, Frank! It's still there. Look!'

And there it was: The White Horse Inn. The guest-house where they had spent the summer of 1941.

The narrow, three-storey building with its big bay window facing the sea was looking the worse for wear. But then so were most of the small hotels and boarding houses lined up along the Prom like a jaw full of broken teeth. The paint was peeling from the front door but there were curtains at the windows and in the big bay hung a yellowing card which read: NO VACANCIES.

'Well, here we are,' said Bill.

And here they were . . . where it had all begun for them on that terrible September night four years before.

'Remember old Burford?' said Frank.

'Course I do. Him and his Ivor Novello on the gramophone all day long!'

'"We'll gather lilacs . . ." that was the song he used to play.'

'Fancy you remembering that! Yes, that was the song. Seems like another world, doesn't it, Frank?'

'It was.'

Bill nodded. 'Yes, you're right, old son. And gone for ever. Least, let's hope so. Still, I'm glad we came back for a last look. Come on, we've got to find a place on the Prom before the parade starts.'

Alec Thrale and his wife had found a place opposite the dais where the American general was going to take the salute. They stood arm-in-arm waiting. Mill had gone up the High Street in search of some ice-cream for them all.

But she was not far from their thoughts. She seldom was these days.

'I worry for her, Alec,' said Vera, 'I do. I catch her eye sometimes and there's such sadness there.'

'Leslie?'

She nodded. 'Mill's become such a dear person. She deserves to be happy.'

'Guilt, that's what it is. On Leslie's part. Crippling guilt.'

'Oh, she's forgiven him long ago. She forgave him in minutes. Don't you remember her down on her knees in our yard calling after him? Calling enough to break your heart. She's forgiven him, Alec.'

'He en't forgive himself, Vera. And till he do there's not a blind thing we can do about it.' Alec took out his watch. 'Won't be long now,' he said.

'Look at people's faces!' said Vera. 'Oh, Alec, what a day! Did you ever doubt it would come?'

'No,' her husband replied. 'But I sometimes wondered if I'd be alive to see it.'

'It mustn't happen again, Alec—not ever. Surely the world's learnt its lesson this time?'

'I'd like to think so, Vera. Though I wouldn't care to swear to it.'

At twelve o'clock precisely the clock tower in the middle of the ornamental gardens began to strike the hour.

In the minutes before, a hush had descended on the crowds lining the pavements either side of the Promenade. Not a silence—people still went on talking, shuffling their feet, straining their necks for a glimpse of movement—but a quiet hush of anticipation. It had descended by no prior arrangement, simply of itself, as though people were gathering themselves. As though, after so long, there was a sudden doubt in everyone's mind that the moment had really come; and they were holding their breath lest something, even at this last minute, should intervene to spoil the promise they'd been made.

Then, on the first stroke of noon, the town band, held there in strict and unbearable silence by the bandleader's baton, crashed into the opening chords of 'Sussex by the Sea'. A great roar went up. The musicians strode forward, and, to wild cheering, the parade fell in behind them: American troops, a contingent of Scouts and Guides, the Fire Brigade, the Lifeboat Crew, and nurses from the

Cottage Hospital. Out in the bay the MTB began to fire tracer bullets into the sky, and the fishing boats set off deafening maroons and flares that coloured the still, blue water as they fell. Church bells began to ring all across the town. And the cheering went on and on and on.

'There's our Bill,' said Edie hoarsely, pointing between the marchers to where Bill and Frank were standing on the opposite side of the road.

'Wave, George,' said Rose, and took her baby's hand.

And Frank and Bill waved back.

Mill Gill came out of the shop. A gang of children were chasing along in the space behind the crowd and as they passed one of them bumped against her and she staggered back against the shop window, struggling desperately to protect the ice-creams. Then, as she recovered herself and prepared to walk on, she became aware of someone watching her. Every other face was turned eagerly towards the Promenade but this one was turned towards her.

She spoke his name. But so quietly that she could hardly hear herself.

''Lo, Mill,' he replied. 'Alec and Vera said you'd be here.'

'Oh, Les . . . Oh, Les,' she said. 'And I thought I'd never see you again.'

'Here I am. Like the bad penny, eh?'

'Don't you say that!' she said fiercely. 'Don't you ever say that. I never gave up hope, Les.'

'For me?'

'Yes.'

'For me, Mill? But, Mill, I done such a bad thing to you.'

'No, you never.'

'I did. To think . . . You know what I thought, don't you?'

'Yes,' she said. 'And I know you couldn't help yourself. I know that cos I know you.' And she placed a hand on his sleeve. 'And, anyway, it don't matter no more. None of it matters. Not now.'

He pushed her hand away. 'It do matter. To me it do,' he said. 'There ain't a day gone by ever since when it ain't mattered. Not to me.'

'I've got you back, Les. Safe and sound. That's what matters.'

'Mill, I'm sorry.'

'It's over, Les. And I've got my little brother back. Come on.' She slipped her hand under his arm. 'Come and meet everyone, eh?' And she began to hurry him back towards the Prom. 'Frank and his dad's here somewhere,' she said. 'And his auntie and all her lot. And Vera and Alec . . . course, you've seen them . . . and . . . and . . . Oh, Les! Les, everybody's here! Everybody's here now!'

As she spoke there was a deafening roar and a loud gasp from the crowd. Some of them ducked instinctively. The band stopped playing and the parade stumbled to a halt as everyone stood and looked up. A gleaming fighter-plane came hurtling down the Promenade, it seemed no more than a few feet above the chimney tops.

When it reached the pier the plane banked out gracefully over the sea. It soared over the water and spun in a perfect Victory Roll, then another, and another and another. Then, as hats were thrown into the air and the cheers began again, it climbed steeply away, faster and faster, climbing higher and higher, until all that remained was a splinter of silver light glinting in the empty blue sky.

Michael Cronin lives in London and has been a profes-
sional actor for the past thirty-five years. He has worked
with theatrical companies throughout the UK, Europe, the
USA, Japan, and Australia. He has appeared frequently in
films and on television, where he is best and most often
remembered as 'Bullet' Baxter, the gym teacher in the
BBC's *Grange Hill*. *In the Morning* is the third book in
Michael's series following the Resistance movements
against the Nazis in Occupied Britain.